POINT TEN ZEROS SIX NINE

AF652564

notionpress.com

POINT TEN ZEROS SIX NINE

Dhiraj Singh

notionpress
.com

Notion Press

Old No. 38, New No. 6

McNichols Road, Chetpet

Chennai - 600 031

First Published by Notion Press 2015

Copyright © Dhiraj Singh 2015

All Rights Reserved.

ISBN: 978-93-52061-58-7

This book has been published in good faith that the work of the author is original. All efforts have been taken to make the material error-free. However, the author and the publisher disclaim the responsibility.

No part of this book may be reproduced or transmitted in any form or by any means, graphic, electronic, or mechanical, including photocopying, recording, taping, or by any information storage retrieval system, without the permission, in writing, from the author.

Printed at BVR Prints, Chennai - 600 005.

Dedicated to my loving and inspirational wife Rashmi; my taller and smarter than me children, Eklavya and Eeshaan; and my dear and strong mother.

ACKNOWLEDGEMENTS

Twists and turns in life are part of fate and destiny. There were many people who helped me during my twists and turns and also helped me directly or indirectly in the writing of this book, and the series. It would be *karmic* injustice if I didn't acknowledge their contribution. Firstly, my wife Rashmi, who was a constant inspiration and reviewer of my books! The second valuable reviewer who never hesitated to give his blunt feedback is my good friend and colleague, Anil Dias. My special acknowledgement of Amitabh Mundhra who is my friend, mentor, and elder brother who always had more faith in me than I did in myself, and was always there to absorb my emotional outbursts! I also wish to thank Rituraj, a very special and inspirational friend and colleague, with whom I can never remain upset for long due to some *karmic* connection!

I would like to thank my other extended family members – my mother, my in-laws, Miki mama, my Jijajis, and of course my younger brother, Nitu – for their constant support and encouragement. My personal friends who supported me unconditionally

– Dhinchak Gang from IIT, and Nimish, Sanjiv and so many others whose support will always be cherished. My business friends who kept faith in me always – Om, Subbu, Brotin, Manoj and many others. My other support groups like Atul / Vasanth, Deepak / Piyush, and Sunil without whose help I would have struggled. A special thanks also to Ray and from whom I still draw motivation and courage.

Last but not the least, a very big thank you to the entire Notion Press team, who pushed me, guided me, and kept running with me, all the way! And a silent thank you to the *Aghori baba* who I met by providence on a flight, and who inspired the title of this book.

1

We sat in the balcony of our apartment in Gurgaon overlooking the beautifully landscaped garden of the condominium. The winter sun was in full glory and shone directly on the radiant and beautiful face of Aashu. I could see the freckle marks and the few faint early signs of wrinkles. They made her look more real and yet ethereal. As she sipped from her first cup of brew that morning, I could see her pink lips relishing the taste of the green tea while I savoured the cocktail taste of the morning sun and the resplendent beauty of Aashu. I looked at the balconies of the other apartments and saw some of our friends basking in the warm winter sunlight. I looked around the vast expanse of the other high-rise buildings nearby and wondered how many others were enjoying a similar experience that morning.

And then my mind went on an overdrive and began calculating the number of people in Gurgaon who could be having a cup of tea with their loved ones at that moment, and then the number of people in the National Capital Region, and then in India, and then the whole world. Then the world too seemed infinitesimally small when I looked up at the sky and the small part of the universe my naked eye could see. If we are just a small planet in a galaxy of billions of planets, in a universe of billions of galaxies, and, possibly, in a multiverse having billions of universes, then am I significant in any way to anybody at all?

"Where are you lost again, Jeetu?" Aashu asked with a hint of irritation in her voice.

"Oh, nowhere. Maybe just in the vast depth of your eyes!" I loved to reel out filmy dialogues when speaking to her.

"Okay, you can continue swimming in my eyes while I start cooking chicken curry for lunch."

No, I was not that insignificant. I had somebody who cared for me, somebody who was willing to sacrifice the pleasure of sitting for half an hour more in the indulgent and rather rare winter sunlight to prepare chicken curry that I loved for Sunday lunch. Aashu got up from her chair and as she turned to open the door of the balcony leading to the house, I could not but steal a quick glance at the shapely mound of flesh below her waist that was tightly wrapped in a green cotton *sari*. She was nearing 40 but could still stir up wild emotions in me. Was it the emotions of the heart carried in small packets of love through the capillaries of the blood stream or was it the often-wild, often-romantic memories of the past and the dreams of the future, carried through the nerve wires of the brain, or was it simply my whole body acting in unison and whispering to every neighbouring cell in the body that Jeetu was still in love, madly and deeply in love.

Love is a strange word. It's the only thing in the world that makes life worth living for, dying for, and killing for.

I was born in a small town called Jamshedpur, currently part of the Jharkhand state in India and at that time part of Bihar. My father was a mechanical engineer working in one of the many Tata companies in Jamshedpur. My mother was a strong and lovely woman who took care of the house and put up with the uneasy rollercoaster ride of my growing-up years.

My paternal grandfather, *baba* as I called him, was a businessman dealing in coal in a village near Dhanbad. Some people tell me that his business was more with the mafia and less with coal. I remember visiting *baba* during my summer holidays. I always came back with fond memories. His house was a palatial double storeyed bungalow painted in glistening red and white colours. It had one large hall in the ground floor, a guest room, and a room for all the support staff (or servants as many like to call them). The upper floor was where my grandfather stayed with my *chachu* (my father's younger brother) and his simple but elegant wife whom we lovingly called *choti chachi*. My grandmother had died at a very young age and I never had the opportunity to play with her. Perhaps *baba* tried to compensate for this by showering a double dose of love and affection on me.

When I was 12 years old, I had been to *baba's* place during the summer holidays. I remember waking up one morning to the shouts of a large crowd outside our place. *Baba* was sitting on a wooden cot with colourful mattresses and a large circular pillow on one side. He rested his elbow on this pillow, smoking from a pipe emanating from a silver plated, glass bottomed green *hookah*. I rushed down in excitement and mingled in the crowd, away from the gaze of *baba*. I soon understood the reason for the gathering.

One of my father's second cousins had a daughter. Neha *didi* was studying arts in her undergraduation from the prestigious St Stephen's College in Delhi. She had fallen in love with a Punjabi boy studying with her in college. The boy's parents were quite happy with this relationship and had accepted Neha *didi* with open arms. They wanted them to get married after college. Neha *didi* came to the village to convince her family. But all hell broke loose when she mentioned he was a Punjabi boy. Her family protested and brought this matter to my *baba* who seemed to wield some influence on such matters.

"This marriage cannot happen. It will bring disrepute to our family. Nobody will marry the other girls in our family after this," shouted a short, dark, pot-bellied woman in her early 50s. She was another distant cousin of my father. I wondered how *she* had got married.

"Silence, silence," *baba* roared. Immediately, there was deafening silence all around. "Family honour and pride is above everything else. There is nothing else more important than this. Pride and honour is worth living for, dying for, killing for." To my young and not-so-innocent mind, this didn't seem to make much sense even then.

"Neha should get married immediately to the young Rajput boy working as a graduate trainee in Tata Steel in Jamshedpur. I know that boy's father. He has helped me in the supply of scrap from Tata Steel."

Ah, so this was a return favour for *baba's* business dealings. But why Jamshedpur, I thought? Now I will have one more relative to visit every second weekend with my parents and touch their feet asking for blessings. I would also have to sit in the living room with my head pointing downwards and occasionally raising it to answer mundane questions such as "Son, what do you want to do when you grow up?" I often wanted to reply, "First, you guys grow up!" But my parents had taught me to show respect to elders.

"So it's decided. Neha will return to Bihar and then be married to this engineer in Jamshedpur before September." *Baba's* words were always regarded as the final verdict and nobody ever dared to debate thereafter.

In one of my later visits to *baba's* village, I was told by some local villagers about another incident that had taken place before my birth, even before my parents had gotten married. One of my aunts (my father's first cousin) used to live in the village. She had fallen in love with *baba's* driver, Ram Singh. Ram Singh was a Rajput but belonged to a poor family. He was happy driving my *baba's* grand white Ambassador car. He had grown to become a trusted confidante of *baba* and was considered part of the family. When and how my aunt and Ram Singh fell in love, nobody knew. But it soon became known to all in the village that this was more than just a passing crush.

The story goes that when *baba* came to know of this, he took Ram Singh out for a drive in the mud road along the river near the village. Somebody heard a gunshot near the road later that day. The next day, Ram Singh's dead body was found with a bullet piercing his right eye and brain, floating in a river near a village 20 km away from *baba's* village.

My aunt was married to a local feudal landlord later that year. She now lives happily with her children and grandchildren in the same village.

I also heard that was the same year my father had decided to leave the village and go to Jamshedpur and take up a job with the Tatas. My logical mind reflected on these sequence of events later in life and my conclusion was that there was a strong correlation between Ram Singh's killing and my father moving to Jamshedpur. I still owe a personal 'thank you' to Ram Singh for this. May his soul rest in peace!

2

Jamshedpur is not heaven or even a Kashmir, but it is not far behind. At least in those days. The near-heaven had clean roads, green parks, great recreational clubs, good schools and best-in-class sports facilities. What I loved the most about Jamshedpur were not the man-made things but what the great designer above had bestowed on this place. The lovely mountains surrounding Jamshedpur were so inspiring and they had perhaps sown the first seeds of my romance in me. The Dalma hills, an elephant sanctuary, was my favourite place in this mini natural paradise of Bihar. The hills stood tall like a protective bodyguard all around Jamshedpur. They could be viewed from the top of the terrace or the balcony of most houses in Jamshedpur. The beautiful Dimna lake, a favourite among picnickers with its blue-green waters, surrounded by the base of the Dalma hills, was like a serene damsel.

With great difficulty, my parents found me a place in the most well-known Jesuit school in Jamshedpur. I still remember that my maternal uncle had invited the school's principal to our house for lunch and convinced him about the virtues of an innocent boy who was about six years old then.

I was a competitive student from the beginning and I soon started to excel in studies. I would get up at 5 a.m. every day on my own to study. Then I got ready to take a bus to school. Discipline, time management, and self-motivation are not things that can be learned from self-help books but they are virtues inculcated by habit and practice. I often wondered how one inculcated these habits without having discipline, time-management and self-motivation! Maybe it's the circumstances that teach you these qualities early on in life. Maybe it's the aspiration for the rewards that come from the practice of such qualities. Maybe it's in one's DNA. Maybe it's *karma* and destiny.

Coming back to school, yes, I was a bright student. But I was also turning out to be a big rebel both at home and school. Whether it was the raging hormones or the desire to stand out in a crowd, I shall never know. But soon I started having strong and intense communication gaps with my father.

"When will you come back from your friend's place? When will you study?" he would often ask. I would reply curtly or, if I was in a good mood, with a fair amount of sarcasm. Sarcasm has a very mysterious impact on most human beings. It's not abusive nor is it derogatory but it leaves a deep scar. It was more like 'scarcasm'. Sarcasm causes deep confusion in the ego cells of the brain, which had not evolved over the past 100,000 years, to deal with the menacing choice and permutation-combination of words. The brain had never perceived this to be a threat to survival and probably never developed a coping mechanism, leading to a confused state of the mind that faces sarcasm.

My father did not know how to react to my sarcasm and took to the most primitive form of self-defence known to mankind – physical reaction. He would often take a small cane or belt and use it with generosity on my back. I gained a lot of sympathy from my girlfriends when I convinced them that the marks on my back were not stretchmarks (which they were) but grim reminders of my father's brutality.

Around that time, the movie *Shakti* was playing in the cinema halls. It starred Amitabh Bachchan in the role of a rebel son; his father was played by Dilip Kumar. Now I, like most of India, had a very deep connection with Amitabh Bachchan. But mine was a very different kind of connection. I started to imagine myself as a younger version of Amitabh Bachchan. After every Amitabh movie, I went to the local tailor and got clothes stitched in the same style and colour as that of Amitabh's clothes in the movie, much to the chagrin of my father. But my mother was amused. Clothes maketh a man. And definitely a young man. So there I was – the clothes made me the angry young rebel Amitabh Bachchan of Jamshedpur.

Like Bachchan in his movies, I rebelled against a lot of things – the control of teachers and other staff at school and my father at home. I even fought hard for my love (more on that later). I guess these causes of rebellion hold good even today among the youth globally.

The poor working class fights against the control of the rich capitalists, the Islamic world is trying to fight against the attempts to control by the Western society, the youth is fighting against the control (or sometimes the lack of it) of corrupt politicians and administration. Not to mention, the daily wars waged between the controlling housewife and the housemaid or parents and children. Ironically, there is never a rebellion against the control of the greatest controller of them all – the Supreme One.

Fighting for one's love is more interesting. Love of the traditional kind – for one's life partner, parents, children, siblings and friends – is well understood and appreciated. Most people fight for them. Love for one's own country, his or her motherland, the soil where he or she grew up is also respected and understood. What I don't understand are the fights and rebellions for the love of oil or other natural resources, religion, pure authoritarian power, and lust – these are not fights worth fighting for.

Naturally, I could not fathom the supposed control of my teachers and other Jesuit staff (we used to call them 'Father so and so') at school. And so my fight started.

My *baba* often said, "Son, live life as if every day is Holi and every night Diwali." And I did take that literally. My Maths teacher had to bear the brunt of powdered colour in the petrol tank of his two-wheeler Lambretta and my English teacher had the misfortune of seeing fireworks when washing swabs were burnt in class.

My Hindi teacher often threw my books from my class on the fifth floor to the ground floor after reading my essay or letter. Why? Because somehow I could not find any other name in my love letters than his teenaged daughter's name. My geography teacher was very encouraging and supportive of my understanding of the 'Bo Lons Law' in class when I tried to explain a complex topic on water bodies. He used the same theory to explain this 'concept' in other classes too. Only later did we all realise that there was no such law or theory and was just a figment of imagination. I barely passed geography that year.

3

Love is a more interesting battle to fight and to fight for. My school had been an all-boys school for several decades but due to our good fortune, girls were finally allowed in our school. It was a Eureka moment for all of us. It was as though we had been travelling across a desert for several years with no sight of water and suddenly an ocean appeared right in the middle of the desert. I took this serendipity very seriously and plunged head on into this 'ocean' of opportunity.

Nirupama had joined our school in the same grade as ours. She had just shifted from Bangalore. Her father was a professor at the renowned XLRI Institute in Jamshedpur. Nirupama had grown up in a city bigger than ours and had more liberal views on life than us. She was tall and slender, with a lovely 'wheatish' tanned complexion. Her hair was cut short and she looked lovely in her white shirt and jeans. Actually, she looked lovely in most outfits she wore. On the second day of joining school, I mustered the courage to walk up to her and say, "Hi, are you liking this place?"

"It's very different from Bangalore, but I am sure I will get used to it." She replied with the ease of a Tendulkar long-on drive.

"Do you want to get some *samosas* in the canteen together?" I was getting bolder.

"Sure, let's go." She was bold too.

As we walked to the canteen, I could see the awe-struck envious eyes of my friends and enemies alike. It was a walk I will never forget. It was the walk of coming of age, the walk of a king after conquering a new kingdom, the walk of a mountaineer reaching the summit, the walk of Amitabh Bachchan showing to the world that he could do romantic roles with the ease with which he did action flicks.

The following weekend, I plucked a pink rose flower from my neighbour's garden, placed it in the middle of my history book, and passed it on to Nirupama through one of her friends. She blushed as she saw the flower and returned a 'thank you' note written on a piece of paper through the same friend. Yes, we had become a couple. That's the most any boy in Jamshedpur would have dared to go and I felt proud of that. Till two weeks later.

Nirupama had a boyfriend in her neighbourhood. But I was not aware of this. Two weeks later, I decided to go to her house and introduce myself to her parents or my 'would-be in laws'. But I found Nirupama taking a stroll in a nearby park with a tall, dark and handsome guy. I first thought he could be her brother and went near them to say hello to him. It didn't take long for both of us to realise that we were competitors in the same battlefield. The problem was that I had landed in the enemy's camp all alone, with no preparation whatsoever.

Nirupama quickly excused herself and went home. Her boyfriend soon called his brother and a few other strong-looking friends from the neighbourhood. I knew this was not looking good. I tried a valiant last-minute Amitabh Bachchan act. "I know I will get beaten today but the first one who attacks me will surely land in hospital," I proclaimed. I thought this would dissuade them from attacking me. But they all advanced together and pounced on me a like a pack of dogs. I had never been beaten in public before and that too so ruthlessly. They kicked me in places I never imagined existed. I tried to save myself by placing my hands on my face and head. After about half an hour of pounding, I was allowed to leave with a stern warning never to be seen again near Nirupama or her neighbourhood.

Now, ego is a strange phenomenon. This three-letter-word packs more punch into every cell of the body than any other stimulant (other than love perhaps). The ego first takes over the brain and covers it in a layer of invisible dark matter, which then unleashes its control on the rest of the body. Then, through a finely regulated mechanism, ego injects a large amount of dark energy into every cell of the body. This dark energy allows the body to do exceptional things. I have often wondered why modern scientists wasted so much time studying dark matter and dark energy of this universe.

I took the next bus to Dhanbad and reached *baba's* village. From my sudden unannounced appearance and the bruises on my body, he could quickly piece together everything.

He asked me, "How many were there?"

"7-8 I think," I replied.

Baba called Bhola Yadav, his 6-feet-3-inches-tall body builder personal henchman. He asked him to take along two or three men and go with me to Jamshedpur the next day. I was a man in a hurry and asked them to come with me that afternoon itself.

Upon reaching Jamshedpur, I immediately went to Nirupama's house and called her out. It must have been about 7 in the evening and she was a bit surprised to see me. I had a dagger in my hand and she shrieked seeing it. I asked her for the address of her boyfriend. Reluctantly, she pointed out the place.

Bhola Yadav went up the short flight of stairs to this house and rang the bell. An old lady came out. She went inside to send the tall, dark, handsome boyfriend of Nirupama. As soon as he came out, he realised that I was not there to make friends with him. Apparently, Bhola Yadav was a known name in Jamshedpur. (I was later told by some of my friends that he had a long history of being the biggest ruffian in Jamshedpur till a few years ago when he moved to join my *baba's* business). As soon as Bhola introduced himself to the boy, he started shaking. He folded his hands and started apologising, saying that he had no idea who I was. But a hurt ego is more in pain than a bruised body. And the only way to dissipate the dark matter in the brain was to unleash the dark energy on the person causing the entire dark phenomenon.

And so, with all my might, I jumped and landed a heavy fist on the face of my tormentor. He cried out and landed on the ground with a thud. I kicked him in the groin and then let Bhola Yadav and his men take over. I heard later that the boy had to spend two days in hospital. Everything was settled and I decided never to talk to Nirupama again.

4

Neha *didi* finally did get married to the engineer in Jamshedpur. I attended the wedding. I was part of the group that had to receive the *baraat* from the groom's side. I was standing there at the gate of the Beldih grounds where the ceremony was to take place. I was wondering what was going through Neha *didi's* mind. I decided to go the women's room where she was getting decked in a heavily embroidered Banarasi *sari*.

"Neha *didi*, you are looking lovely."

"Hi Jeetu. Yes, life is indeed very lovely."

I could sense a bit of sarcasm in her reply.

As I heard the sound of gunshots being fired, I realised that the *baraat* was already here. I rushed towards the gate and picked a set of garlands and quickly scanned the incoming tsunami of gun-firing, dancing, and screaming wave of happy faces. We were supposed to place the garlands around the necks of at least five people from the groom's side. As was the practice, the women were not part of the *baraat*. This allowed the men to have a paid vacation of eating, drinking, and enjoying all kinds of debauchery that normally would not have been allowed.

"*Pranaam*, welcome uncle."

"*Pranaam*, welcome *dada ji*."

I was keen to finish my round of five garlands quickly. I heaved a sigh of relief when I did. The *baraat* moved inside the grounds and they were served a glass of cool drink (Thumbs Up or Limca were in demand the most) along with two *samosas*, some chips, and a cashew sweet. They were then seated around a stage on which there were two red chairs that looked more suitable for a king and a queen. Soon, Neha *didi* was escorted to the stage and she sat on the chair next to the groom. The whole crowd went into raptures. But thankfully there were no gun shots this time. Maybe they were all busy finishing their *samosas* and sweets.

Neha *didi* was then expected to place the garland around the groom's neck. The groom was supposed to evade this, as part of the ceremony. The first attempt was unsuccessful. So was the second. And then almost on cue, everyone aligned at the right angles and the garland was successfully placed. It reminded me of the basketball games in school when the ball finally reached the basket on the third attempt.

The other ceremonies were too boring and detailed for me to remember. But I do remember the entertainment laid out for the *baraat*. There was a large tent near the ground. I had dared to venture into the tent around midnight. I still vividly remember a young, round-faced, and innocent-looking girl in a *ghagra choli* gyrating wildly to *Rambha ho, samba ho*, a famous dance song of that time. The wild pack of holidaying men were throwing wads of one rupee notes on her. The more adventurous ones decided to show off their masculinity by firing their guns in the air. Next morning, I tried to count the number of holes in the top cover of the tent but it was too difficult.

I went back home early next morning. I was glad to see my father taking out his motorcycle to work. I could now sleep through the whole morning without any disturbance.

"Son, you must be tired. Shall I give you some *kheer*?" My mother was concerned that I may have lost a lot of energy carrying out the wedding chores. She was eager to replenish it. Why do mothers always want to overfeed their children? Do they feel happy taking care of their children or do they actually think food will do their children good? Or is it the best way to ensure the strength of the mother-son bond that gradually weakens with every new hormone produced in the rapidly growing male body.

So, I had my *kheer* and went to bed. I had had a good time at the wedding. Perhaps someday, I would have a similar ceremony. But my wife would be more beautiful and definitely taller, I thought, and went into deep slumber.

At about 2 p.m., I woke up with a startle as I heard my father shouting. "Will you spend your whole life sleeping? You are a burden on this world and your parents. Why don't you go and join the army? At least you will be of some use to this land."

My father always thought it would be easier for me to pass the National Defence Academy examinations rather than the entrance examinations to IIT, in which I was more interested.

I decided then and there that my life was not going to be a waste. I shall prove my father wrong one day, I vowed.

I studied hard for my class 10 board examinations and I was among the top rankers in school. But life has a strange way of catching up with one's past deeds. Later on in life I learnt this was one's *karma*.

My reputation of being a bit of a *goonda* didn't help me at all while trying to secure admission into the 'plus two' grade. I wasted three months trying to convince different schools to take me but they would do a reference check on me and politely decline.

Finally, my father had to turn to a friend of his who was a trustee at a mediocre school in Jamshedpur. And he had to pull all his weight and give enough assurances over a lunch at home to secure my admission. Life had not changed much over past the 10 years. A lunch had secured my admission into the entry grade and again another lunch had come to my rescue. I have since then never ignored the importance of lunches in my life.

The next two years at this new school was a breeze, largely because I hardly attended school. But I prepared very diligently for my IIT entrance examinations and secured a good enough rank to get a seat in the civil engineering department at IIT Bombay, as it was known then. Since then, any *goonda* with a strong academic record was referred to as a 'Jeetu type case' while being considered for admission.

5

Bombay is where Amitabh Bachchan lived. This made my decision to opt for IIT Bombay quite easy. IIT Kharagpur was the other option. But I didn't really like the distinct possibility of my father dropping by at my college every other weekend. So, I took the Gitanjali Express from Jamshedpur to Bombay and landed there at the start of the monsoons.

The monsoons and I have always had a love-hate relationship. During my school days in Jamshedpur, I used to the love the '4 o'clock' rains. It was so called because of the uncanny habit of the rains to start pouring at around 4 p.m. during most of the monsoon period. It rained for about half an hour and made the weather pleasant enough for us to go out and play cricket. When we grew older, we would take a tour of the lanes of the city where the pretty girls lived, on our bicycles.

On the rare occasions when it rained later at night, I would ask my mother to serve me dinner under an umbrella that I held with one hand while I ate my food with the other hand. This was probably an inspiration from a scene from one of the movies I had seen around that time.

On some lazy early afternoons when it rained, I would sit on the ledge of our balcony and watch the rain-drops race against each other on the electric wires. I would place my bets on the drops that would win the race.

I used to love the monsoons in Jamshedpur. But when I landed in Bombay, I started to hate them.

The monsoons in Bombay were not some light showers or torrential rains for just half an hour. They were like the buzz of a bee constantly hovering near your ear. It never seemed to stop.

There was greenery all around the IIT Bombay campus. During the incessant rains, the foliage only made the campus look gloomy. It had the haunted look of a beautiful face ravaged by perpetual tears.

For the first time I saw so many high-rise buildings all around. And the monsoons covered most of the buildings with a light green algae coating. I didn't like the monsoons in Bombay.

As I looked outside from my room in the hostel, I could see the rain battering the narrow roads inside the campus and the trees lining the roads. The sky looked dark and gloomy.

There were dark clouds everywhere. Life looked different now. The rains no longer seemed romantic to me. It was as though nature was not happy that I was in Bombay and was keen on showing its displeasure with full fury.

"Freshie, come here," shouted a senior standing outside my room. I knew what awaited me. Maybe the senior's ragging would be better than the ragging of the raging rain, I thought. Ragging was a natural part of the overall education at IIT. But I was obviously not prepared for such an education.

"Yes, what's up?" I questioned my senior.

"Son of a bitch, you dare to question me back?"

And I felt a tight slap on the right side of my face.

My first instinct was to slap him back tightly. And my second deliberated post-instinct thought was to call up *baba* and ask him to send Bhola Yadav here. Fortunately, I did neither.

I soon realised that it was in my personal interest to make friends with the seniors than to antagonise them in any way. It was just a few years ago that I had been slapped by a stranger and I had chosen to settle the matter in the manner in which America dealt with troublesome countries – you hurt me, I hurt you double. And now I was slapped again by a stranger and I chose to settle the matter in the manner in which India tackled its neighbouring countries – you hurt me, I will still befriend you.

I soon made peace with the new life and the new weather. I found a close group of friends at my hostel as well as in my department. Ramky was one of them.

Ramky was an Andhraite from the coastal town of Machilipatnam. He was the only son of his parents who were both teachers at a local school. Ramky was a simple person and probably one of the most brilliant minds that I had come across.

Ramky and I grew very close over the next few months at IIT. After our second semester examinations at the end of the first year, Ramky and I decided to hit the local Sujata bar early in the afternoon itself.

"*Yaar*, what is life really about?" Ramky asked after his second bottle of Haywards 10000 beer. Haywards 10000 was the preferred beer of many of us due to its high alcohol content.

"Life is all about enjoying," I said after gulping down my third full bottle in true 'bottoms up' style.

"No, Jeetu, life is more than that. Life is about loving someone so deeply that one forgets the hardships and pains."

As usual, Ramky had a point.

"But Ramky, it is not easy to find someone you can love so much. And if I do find love, I want to live not just this life with her but the next life too."

"Jeetu, that's why God has created soulmates. And the lucky ones know when they meet their soulmates. My father used to say that a soul gets 84 lakhs lives before merging with the Supreme One. And seven of those lives are as human beings. And so do you know the probability of being in the same human lifetime as your soulmate? Its point ten zeros six nine or 0.000000000069 %!"

"Ah, so it is 10 times harder than making out in the 69 position." As usual, I tried in vain to be funny whenever I could not match the brainpower of Ramky.

Alcohol and human beings have a similar origin, dating billions of years ago, much before both were even born. Carbon atoms floating in the universe combined with hydrogen, oxygen and nitrogen to form living organisms. The same carbon atoms also combined with hydrogen and oxygen later to form the dearly loved alcohol. So, we are not too distant cousins actually. And that's why we enjoy, laugh and open up so much when we meet our cousins. Ramky and I were enjoying the company of our close cousins.

After finishing 12 bottles of the powerful beer between us, we could no longer hold the liquid in our bladders. We went to the usual public lavatory for releasing our pain – a drain that ran parallel to the front wall of the IIT campus. We both stood next to each other and sang the friendship song *Yeh dosti hum nahin chodenge,* as we enjoyed the gradual release of pressure.

I zipped up and looked towards Ramky but I could see no one there. Suddenly I heard a faint whimper of the second line of the song *Todenge dum magar tera saath na chodenge* coming from below me. I looked down and saw that Ramky had fallen flat on his back in the drain in front of us. Alcohol is a fun-loving cousin but it can also make a fool of us when not handled with care.

6

I eagerly looked forward to the summer holidays at the end of the first year. I had made a lot of plans for the summer. I was really good at that – planning. People say Librans are good at planning and I too shared the trait. But no matter how many plans you make in life, there is a master planner above who often has other plans.

Fortunately this time, my plans seemed to be in sync with those of the master planner. I boarded the train from Bombay to Jamshedpur and after almost 36 hours of travel through several states of India, I could see the train cross the bridge over the Kharkhai river. The bridge was the connecting point of the industrial suburbs of Jamshedpur to the main town. There is always a sweet feeling of old memories, old sounds, and old smells that filled the mind and body whenever one returned to the city where he or she grew up as a child. I loved that feeling every time.

I saw my father waiting at the railway station in the blistering heat of the summer. After getting admitted to IIT, I had managed to gain a huge jump in respect from my father.

He smiled broadly as he saw me get down from the train and waved to me. I went to him and touched his feet to seek his blessings. I could feel more warmth this time when he said *jeete raho beta*.

After a few days of just sleeping and eating, I realised my summer holidays were not going as per my plans. One fine morning, I decided take a more meaningful path. I packed my bags and told my mother that I was going to spend a few days with *baba* at his village. I could see a tinge of disappointment on my mother's face but she asked me to have breakfast and then go.

I reached *baba's* village in the early afternoon. *Baba* always greeted me as if I was a king. Maybe I indeed was. The king of his heart. *Chachu* and *choti chachi* knew this and they felt happy whenever I came to visit – they knew *baba* would be in a happy mood as long as I stayed.

Baba immediately called out for Bhola.

"Bhola, now Jeetu is in college. He must get special treatment this time. I am entrusting you with the job of teaching him the new lessons of life he needs to know."

This was going as per my plan. I knew what that meant.

I always had a huge fascination for *baba's* special cupboard in which guns and pistols of different kinds were kept. I saw Bhola often cleaning them, polishing them, putting oil or grease in them, and looking down the empty barrels of the guns. *Baba* knew about my fondness for guns but he always asked me to be patient. I had patiently waited for my time. And I guessed this was my time now.

There was a minor hiccup in my plans though.

Bhola brought out a timid looking air gun from somewhere in the cupboard.

"Jeetu sir, this is something for you to start your practice with," he said, almost mockingly I thought.

I knew I could not argue with *baba* if he had made up his mind. I grudgingly took hold of the air gun and looked at it up and down. It was a well-crafted weapon made of wood and iron. It was not as menacing as the double barrel guns I had hoped for but it was not a cute looking toy either. It had real pellets that could actually hurt or even kill small living beings such as birds and rabbits.

I was shocked beyond belief hearing Bhola's suggestion for shooting practice.

"Jeetu sir, I will put this plastic doll on my head. And you have to shoot it."

What! Did he actually mean what he said? Surprisingly, he actually meant it.

Bhola was born and raised in the outskirts of Jamshedpur, somewhere near a place called Jugsalai. He was the only son of his parents who worked as casual labourers in the Tata Steel plant. He had no formal education as a child. But he was always a strong person, in mind and body. He spent a lot of time practising wrestling in the *akhara* near his one bedroom house.

Very early on in his life, he had taken a vow of celibacy. He never married or had any relationship with a woman in his entire life. After both his parents died of illness within a span of two years, he had nothing to worry about or lose in life.

During one of the events at the *akhara* just before the Ramnavami festival, Bhola was spotted by the local scrap mafia lord, Raghuvar Pandey. Raghuvar was a terror in Jamshedpur and the neighbouring areas. The police did not dare mess with him. He had the protection of a few powerful politicians in Patna.

Raghuvar asked Bhola to start working with him. Thus began the most profitable period for the scrap mafia in Jamshedpur. Bhola soon rose up the ranks in Raghuvar's gang and became one of the closest confidantes of Raghuvar.

The politics in Patna took a turn and a new government was formed. Within three months of the formation of the new government, Raghuvar was killed by the police in an encounter attack while he was driving with his family to Dimna lake for a picnic on the first of January.

Bhola knew he would be next on the list soon. He had known *baba* for some years now as they used to do some business together. *Baba* invited him to join him and shift to his village near Dhanbad.

As I stood there with my air gun aiming at the doll on Bhola's head, I remembered Bhola's background, which my mother had told me about recently. What if I missed and shot his forehead? What if he got killed? Yes, this was stupid. Maybe this was Bhola's way of showing that he trusted me fully. Or maybe this was his way of challenging destiny which had not been very fair to him so far.

I had fear in my eyes. He had playful joyfulness in his eyes. When fear is overcome by the mind, it spreads joy to all parts of the body. And when the mind is overcome by fear, it leads to a breakdown of all the mental and physical faculties of the entire body.

I was not going to be afraid today. I took my first shot and hit the doll right in the naval area.

"Bravo, Jeetu sir! You are indeed your *baba's* grandson!" Bhola shouted with glee.

I took 20 more shots that day and hit the doll 19 times with accuracy. The one time I missed – the pellet had whizzed past Bhola's ears but destiny was kind to Bhola this time.

7

Baba was fond of hunting. He often went hunting in the Chota Nagpur forest, a two-and-half hour drive from his village. He was quite happy shooting some wild birds or maybe a rabbit. When lucky, he would return with a deer or a wild boar. He was known for his hunting prowess as much as his business acumen.

One day, I crept beside *baba's* cot while he was sleeping on the terrace enjoying the lazy afternoon. Gently pressing his feet, I mustered the courage to stutter, "*Baba*, hmm… can you, can you take me hunting with you once?" *Baba* had a smile on his face. A smile that seemed to say, "Son, I look forward to passing the baton to you now."

Next early morning, at about 5 a.m., we left for the Chota Nagpur forest in *baba's* Ambassador car. Bhola was with us driving the car. The road to the Chota Nagpur forest was beautiful with acres of yellow mustard fields on both sides of the road. Upon reaching the forest area, we parked the car. We had to ride a bullock cart to go inside the forest.

Baba, Bhola, and I climbed on the back-side of the bullock cart driven by a local villager. *Baba* had his double barrelled Ichhapur manufactured gun with him and he started to load it with 12 bore cartridges. It was about 9 a.m. and the mud track in the forest was wet due to the rare downpour the previous day. The sun was largely hidden by the clouds and it was much darker inside the forest. The dense cluster of sal trees in this dry deciduous forest was filtering out the sunlight further. It looked like early evening.

Baba and Bhola were vigilantly looking around for the first kill of the day. We went deeper into the forest for an hour or so. The track was getting narrower and I could feel adrenaline rushing through every pore and every cell of my body. The nearby shrubs and trees seemed to be whispering silently into our ears. The bells around the necks of the bullocks chimed hauntingly. I moved closer to *baba*.

We were near an area with large bamboo trees. The bamboo trees were about 10 metres in height and the stem diameter was more than 10 cm. I had never seen such a dense gathering of bamboo trees before and I looked at them with awe.

"Sshh... silent," said *baba,* gesturing at Bhola and me. I could hear a slight crackle of grass on the ground from inside the bamboo tree cluster. And within seconds, lo and behold, there was a majestic Royal Bengal tiger, more than 12 feet from head to tail, standing directly in front of us on the mud track. There was no time to think, no time to marvel the glory of this magnificent beast. The mafia and coal business jungles had taught both *baba* and Bhola that only a weak man hesitates. If you see danger, you have to react. If you can be killed, you have to kill it first. *Baba* immediately pointed his gun towards the tiger and shot it in the forehead. The tiger slumped dead to the ground immediately.

"*Baba*, can I touch it?"

"Wait for a minute."

I got down from the cart and went near the tiger. It lay there motionless. It was its *karma* to have emerged suddenly right in front of us. I felt a strange mix of thrill and sadness as I gently touched the tiger's skin. This was not our plan. This was part of the master's plan.

"I have always wanted to hunt a tiger." Bhola grumbled at not having shot the tiger himself.

"You will have your chance one day Bhola, for sure," *baba* predicted.

8

The rest of the summer flew very quickly. Most of the time I was busy bragging about the tiger *WE* had killed. I became more popular among all my younger cousins in Jamshedpur. I was a hero to many of them. And the aunties looked at me somewhat differently now. I was no longer a young adorable kid. I was a man now.

My father was certainly not too pleased with this adventure and let his feelings be known to my mother.

"You should not have let him go there. He does not know the dangers in the village and in the forests. You should not pamper him so much that he actually starts to think of himself as Jim Carwet." (My father had not read much about Jim Corbett but had heard his stories).

I had to catch the evening train back to Bombay. My father had come to drop me off. Once I climbed the coach, I asked him to leave. He blessed me with tears swelling in his eyes. I hid my tears bravely. I had just hunted a tiger. How could I let tears get in the way of my new-found status as a manly hero? I turned around and went inside the coach to find my seat.

I had reserved the lower berth so that I could enjoy the views from the window throughout the journey. I looked at my ticket again. Yes, the seat number was correct. But there was a middle-aged man sitting there with two large suitcases on the seat.

"Uncle, this is my seat. Can you please get up immediately and let me sit?"

"Son, just wait for a couple of minutes. My daughter has gone to sort out our tickets with the ticket collector and will be here any moment."

"Sorry Uncle. But I have to place my luggage and I can't keep waiting."

I was getting impatient. Most of us who have all the time in our homes but as soon as we hit the roads in our vehicles or get into a train, bus or aeroplane, we become the busiest people on the planet. And I was certainly looking very busy and impatient that day. Maybe I was restless about something. Maybe there was something in the air.

I was right. I soon sensed a subtle cocktail aroma of fresh roses mixed with butterscotch and stirred in vanilla extract. I turned around and saw a pink cheeked girl with smooth, long, black hair wearing a yellow *salwar kurta*. She had a kind and gentle face with lips that smiled as well as teased you simultaneously. Her nose was perfect and seemed to have been planted by the maker at the end of his sculpture. She had an athletic body with all the right curves. Her skin had a few light freckles but you could notice them only when you were not blinded by the pinkish glow on her face.

"Hey mister, you don't need to be so rude to my father," she said.

Obviously, the man sitting on my seat was her father.

"Uh...uh... I was only asking..."

"We have got our tickets confirmed now. *Dadu*, please sit on the opposite seat on the lower berth. It has been confirmed. I have got the upper seat."

She looked at me once more with a tinge of disgust. She sat beside her father who was now sitting next to another person near the window. I sat adjacent to the window on the opposite side. I sheepishly glanced at her once and quickly looked the other way. She seemed normal now. Normal in her behaviour but exquisite in her looks.

"I am sorry for speaking to you like this. Hi, my name is Aashana Verma. My friends call me Aashu," she said to me.

"Oh, don't bother. It was my fault. My name is Jeetendra Singh. My friends and family call me Jeetu."

9

A train journey is one of the most enjoyable experiences in life. I like to just gaze at the beauty outside the window. But not today. The beauty was inside the window today. I took every opportunity to look inside the compartment, as I adoringly caressed her beautiful face with my eyes. I knew what Ramky had meant. This was my point ten zeros six nine per cent moment. Either I could seize it or wait for another moment or another lifetime that may never come.

"Aashu, where are you coming from?"

"We live in Calcutta. And we are coming from there. But our tickets were to be confirmed in Jamshedpur only. So the confusion."

As if taking a cue, she continued.

"I am going to join the economics course in Bombay at St Xavier's College. The classes start from next week. *Dadu* is coming with me to Bombay as he has some business meeting there."

Dadu was her *papa*. Well, my *papa* was my *dadu*.

"That's great. I study in Bombay too. At IIT Powai. Have you ever been there?"

I was hoping the conversation would continue for a little more while at least.

"Oh yes, I had been there last year during your annual festival while on a holiday with a cousin. I was quite amazed. But it is not my type."

My type? What type? Did she mean the institute, the festival, or the students there?

I could not leave this to chance.

"Sorry, your type for what?"

She laughed aloud. I saw her laughing for the first time. Her beautiful but uneven white teeth were visible as she had a full and heartfelt laughter. I wish I could laugh like that. I rarely laughed openly and loudly. A good laugh originates deep down inside the body and then travels all the way up to the mouth and face, gathering magnitude and intensity along the way. I could see Aashu's laugh gather all the intensity and magnitude, and it seemed to have originated from the heart.

"I meant I don't like these kind of festivals. The noise and crowd gets to me."

"Well, next time you visit the campus, I shall show you places where there is hardly any noise and definitely no crowd."

I had taken a shot at the doll. I hoped it would hit the target.

"Yes, why not Jeetu? I would love to do that sometime."

"*Dadu*, do you want your dinner now?" She quickly unpacked a plastic box containing potato curry and *parathas*.

They had their dinner. I too unpacked the delicious *aloo parathas* and mango pickle, wrapped in aluminium foil, which my mother had prepared for me.

After dinner, I saw Aashu climb up to the upper berth and lay out a thin white bedsheet on the seat. She went to sleep soon with her face pointing at the partition separating the other compartment from ours. I too lied down and turned off the lights. I had difficulty falling asleep. My eyes kept wandering up to see her face.

All through the next day, we hardly talked. She preferred to spend time in her upper berth reading magazines and books.

As the train stopped at Kalyan station, I nodded to her and meekly said, “Bye Aashu. Hope to see you sometime.”

She smiled and nodded.

I stepped down from the train. I had a double pang of separation this time – of missing my family and Aashu. I cursed myself for not having talked more to her and asking for details to meet later. Had I wrecked my chance? Or was I just being too optimistic? Maybe she had a boyfriend?

I went back to my hostel with these thoughts. I knew life would not be the same again.

10

Durga *puja* was in early October that year. I always looked forward to it. This was one of the most important festivals in Jamshedpur, celebrated with great enthusiasm and passion. There was a sizeable population of Bengalis living in Jamshedpur and they spent a full month planning for this event. Even for the rest of us, this was a very exciting time of the year. We went to all the *pandals* to have *gol gappas* and devil's egg *chaap*. We met our friends and admired the beauty of the young girls clad in traditional red and white *saris*.

I asked a Bengali friend from my hostel to guide me about the good *pandals* to visit in Bombay during Durga *puja*.

"*Dada*, there are many. Where do you want to go?"

I had forgotten this was Bombay, not Jamshedpur. And I had only 3-4 hours on Sunday.

"Just the nearest ones perhaps."

"Then you must visit the one near Powai market. And one in Ghatkopar."

I had an early lunch at the mess on Sunday and rushed towards the main gate to catch a bus to

Ghatkopar. I had planned to visit the Ghatkopar *pandal* first and then the Powai *pandal* in the evening.

The *pandal* was lovely. It resembled the Victoria Memorial *pandal* in Calcutta. The Durga goddess idol loomed large in the *pandal,* which was teeming with people in bright clothes and big smiles. The aroma of the incense sticks near the stage brought back memories of my school years. It is strange how an aroma or the weather or some songs suddenly excite dormant parts of your memory. There was deafening *dhak* beats from the large drum that hung around the necks of men who were beating its sides with thin wooden sticks. Some young boys and girls were dancing wildly, yet in a strangely rhythmic manner, to the beats.

I was lost in this wondrous display of religious fervour when suddenly I felt it again. The same feeling that I had had in the train compartment while returning from my summer vacation. I looked around and saw Aashu enter the *pandal* with a woman friend.

Aashu was wearing a pink *sari* with a matching long sleeve blouse and looked divine. I immediately apologised in my heart to Goddess Durga for being more reverent to Aashu at that time. But Aashu was looking no less than a goddess herself.

"Hi Aashu! What a pleasant surprise to find you here." I waved to her and went towards her.

She did recognise me instantly, and for a moment I thought I saw a sparkle in her light brown eyes.

"Hi Jeetu! What are you doing here?"

"Waiting to get a glimpse of the most beautiful goddess, I guess." I wished to God that I would stop using such cheesy filmy phrases whenever I was tormented by the hormones of the heart.

She laughed out aloud – the same laughter, the same innocence I had been dreaming about for months after I first met her.

Her friend said 'hi' to me and then taking the unspoken hint from both Aashu and me, she politely excused herself.

We both sat down on bright red plastic chairs inside the *pandal*. I could feel the gaze of some elders in the *pandal*. But today I was not going to stop.

"Aashu, I have often thought about you after we first met in the train."

"Yes, that was quite a strange way to meet *na*?"

"That is what is called destiny, maybe. And maybe it was orchestrated by Durga *ma* herself!"

The laugh again. It served as the biggest catalyst for the chemicals going crazy in my heart and mind.

"Can I take you out for a cup of coffee nearby?"

"Why not, Jeetu? I would like that. Let me just tell my friend and then we can go."

I could not believe this. Ramky, you mad genius, I thought. Your probability theory has no meaning when destiny and Durga *ma* have other plans.

11

Aashu and I started to meet more often. Sometimes at her college canteen or sometimes at Juhu Chowpaty. Sometimes at the IIT campus or sometimes at Marine Drive. We would talk about our families, our school days, our future aspirations, our friends at college, our frustration with the politicians, and, of course, our mutual love for movies.

Our favourite meeting point was the theatre, especially Odeon in Ghatkopar. We were both movie buffs. We enjoyed watching movies together – popcorn in one hand and a Thumbs Up bottle in the other. I liked the way Aashu would snuggle close to me while watching movies and clasp my arms tightly whenever there was a tense moment in the movie.

Once, we were watching *Maine Pyaar Kiya*, a huge hit of those times, at Odeon. A popular line used by the actor and actress in the movie was "*Pyaar mein no sorry, no thank you*." (In love, there is no need to say 'sorry' or 'thank you'.)

"Jeetu, we must also no longer say 'sorry' or 'thank you' to each other now," Aashu said with a slightly shy smile, twirling the curls of her long black hair with her delicate fingers.

"Are you sure, Aashu? Hope it is not because of the impact of this movie."

"No, I mean it Jeetu. I think I am in love with you."

"I don't *think* so, Aashu. I KNOW, I am madly in love with you!'

There was an almost unbearable urge at that moment to lean across and kiss Aashu to celebrate this mutual acceptance of love with the stamp of a physical bond. But we were aware of other people around. Love is a beautiful and special package personally made by the grand designer above, within which lies deep affection and care for each other, a strong sense of respect for each other, and a healthy dose of physical lust for each other.

So, while our feelings of affection and lust for each other were overwhelming at that moment, our respect for each other helped us put the brakes on it. I could not see her getting embarrassed in front of others. I wanted her to be comfortable when she was physically intimate with me. I wanted her to enjoy the physical moments and not get nervous. I wanted her to smile and laugh when I tickled her 'love' bones. I took a vow that day that I would be forever selfless in love.

"Where are you lost, my Jeetu?" asked Aashu, as she intertwined her fingers with mine.

I was hers now. She called me hers. There isn't a more satisfying feeling than that – belonging to somebody who does not share your DNA.

I looked at her and then turned to the screen and said, "Isn't the heroine phenomenally beautiful?"

She slapped me lightly on my shoulders as if she was reading my mind.

We walked out of the main gate of the theatre with a broad smile on our faces. The guard at the main gate, who was quite familiar to us by now, smiled at us. We both said 'thank you' to him almost simultaneously. The 'thank you' was not for the movie but for guarding the place where we made our first sacred pledge of love to each other.

We both walked together till the bus stand. Her bus was about to leave. She turned around and hugged me closely. We then said 'bye' to each other with a lump in our throats and a warm ache in our hearts. She slowly walked towards the bus and started to climb the steps to get inside the bus. I wanted her to turn around and look at me once. At the first step, she didn't turn around. Not on the second step either. As she was about to take the third step, she turned around slightly and her eyes searched for me. She saw me waiting at the same place she had left me; she smiled her most radiant smile and waved again.

I have often wondered if I had shared this incident with anybody from the movie industry for years later a blockbuster movie carried a similar scene.

12

Ramky was not too keen to hear my story.

"Jeetu, this is too soon for real love to happen. It's more of lust. You need to really understand a person and know her deeply to fall in love. If there is no depth, how can you fall in love, my friend? See the logic?" I didn't know if Ramky was in a literary or humorous mood or was just plain sarcastic.

The weather was getting a bit cold. The nights were a bit chilly. Nothing compared to the cold of Jamshedpur but you could still feel the drop in temperature. And this was an ideal time for viruses to prowl and feed on their unsuspecting and helpless prey. I soon became their prey.

It was terrible. I was lying on my cot in my hostel room for two days with a nasty headache and a running nose. I felt sudden shivers too. I was taking some medicine prescribed by a friend's father who was a doctor in the Vikhroli area of Bombay.

I still can't figure out why one wants to have his or her near and dear ones nearby when ill. The same near and dear ones seem to cause headaches otherwise. I guess it's the feeling of vulnerability or the need to feel wanted and cared for. Or maybe it was a desire to see them one last time should God have other plans in store. My conclusion is that it's just the time when one can feel and act like a baby – a stage of life you cannot go back to but can always crave for. I too had this craving.

I asked my room-mate to inform Aashu that I was not well and also tell her to not worry. Deep down I was hoping she would get deeply worried and come running to see me, tend to me, and pamper me. I went to sleep and had a weird dream of Aashu feeding me milk from a bottle.

Next morning at around 6 a.m., I was woken up by a slight knock on the door. I was feeling a little better and stronger now. I quickly got up to open the door. She was there. Dreams do come true.

"Why didn't you inform me earlier?" She admonished me with a deep frown on her face.

"*Arrey,* sit down first Aashu. It was no big deal. And I am a grown-up man now. I can look after myself," I said valiantly, trying to not think of my dream last night.

For the next two hours, she kept placing a wet towel on my head and pressing it gently. She had also brought some cookies for me and a bottle of chocolate milk.

"This will make you feel better, Jeetu."

I smiled while I sipped the chocolate milk.

She had to leave for an important class in college. I desperately wanted her to stay. I desperately wanted to kiss her. But I had vowed to be selfless in a physical relationship with Aashu. I could not possibly pass on my horrible viruses to her. I had to wait. And I was sure it would be worth the wait.

13

In a couple of weeks, there was a marathon run sponsored by a leading multinational bank. Aashu wanted to take part in it. She was a regular runner and had represented her college in the 400 metres race. She wanted to test her mental strength and physical stamina by running a marathon.

"Why do you want to do this Aashu? I don't see any point in running miles after miles. Probably it does more damage to your body than any good."

I tried to dissuade her for I feared she wouldn't have enough time for me over the next few days once she started her preparation for the marathon. I was not going to be selfish in the physical aspects of love, but I didn't mind being selfish in wanting more time and attention from her.

"Jeetu, do you know how many miles our ancestors must have run every day thousands of years ago? Don't you think we should at least re-live that experience?" She teased me. I knew once she had made up her mind it was impossible to change it. I am a big believer in taking the middle path of mutual compromise. It makes everyone happy and life goes on without any grudge.

"Okay, Aashu. But at least you can do your preparation at the lovely grounds of the IIT campus? There is so much greenery here and you probably need more oxygen in your lungs. Our ancestors used to have much more oxygen to breathe in those times, *na*?" I looked at her imploringly.

"Hmm... You always have your way, Jeetu. Cool, I will come over to IIT this Saturday but I will not shower in your hostel. I will go to the girl's hostel later and use the facilities there. A sister of my friend lives there. Deal?"

"Deal!"

On Saturday, I went to receive her at the main gate. We walked together to the sprawling green ground on campus. Whenever I walked with Aashu within the IIT campus, I could feel the gaze of both the boys and girls passing by. Given the absurdly low ratio of girls to boys at IIT, I could fully empathise with the boys and understand their stares. But why did the girls stare? Ramky said this was a natural phenomenon of ensuring that God had not been unfair in bestowing both intelligence and beauty on a single person. Once the girls knew that Aashu was neither a student at IIT nor lived in the girls' hostel on campus, they were more relaxed and happy. The girls at IIT may have been satisfied with this, but I was happy that God had indeed been unfair in Aashu's case.

She was wearing a red T-shirt over a tight black track pants. Her hair was tied neatly behind in a ponytail. She did some stretching and smiled at me. She then gave me a stopwatch and a bottle of glucose water.

"Jeetu, just measure the time I take to complete every round and shout it out to me when I cross you."

She started running. As she ran, I could not help noticing her shapely bottom, highlighted by the tight pants. My hormones went berserk again.

After 12 rounds, I could see her starting to sweat profusely. I also knew she would not take a break before completing her target of 30 rounds for the day. But I could not let her body be depleted of the essential minerals and liquids. She had to be fresh and energised even at the end of 30 rounds. My hormones and brain cells were working in tandem and hatching plans, which I was not consciously aware of.

The next time she crossed me, I started running behind her carrying the glucose bottle.

"Jeetu, what are you doing?" She was surprised to see me.

"You need to drink this while running."

She winked at me and took the bottle and gulped down almost a quarter of it. I kept running behind her. When she was satisfied, she handed the bottle back to me. I quickly ran in the opposite direction to get to the starting point. I shouted to her the time she had taken, when she crossed me. I continued this routine over the next hour or so.

At the end of 30 rounds, I announced the total time. I could see she was not happy with it. She was also very tired. The collusion of my hormones and brain cells came into play again.

"Hop on my back, Aashu. I shall carry you over to a beautiful place for some rest."

She hesitated for a moment and then jumped on my back with her arms crossed over my neck for balance. She was sweating. I loved that smell. I could have carried her like this for hours if I had had the strength.

The road across the grounds that led to a secluded and dense forest area was not that far. This place had a small opening amid the dense vegetation at the border of the Powai lake. It was one of my favourite spots on campus. It bordered the Borivali National Park and the Powai lake.

We both lied down enjoying the nature and the silence. The silence of the universe and the space...

When there is no noise or sound, I love listening to the hum of waves from outer space. It gives a strange peace to my inner self.

"Jeetu, someday we should build a house in a forest like this and live there forever."

"Yes and also have our kids growing up there."

I didn't know if this was me speaking or the orchestrated combination of my hormones and brain cells. But it did excite the most passionate instinct in her. The maternal instinct. She got up and held out her hand to help me get up.

We both looked at each other. We knew this was the moment. She leaned forwards and closed her eyes as she parted her luscious pink lips. I grabbed her with both my hands and held her tight, as my lips locked with hers in slow and circular motions. I loved the wetness of her lips and didn't stop kissing her for the next 10 minutes.

When we stopped kissing, we again looked at each other. We then hugged each other for five minutes.

Breaking our blissful moment was a loud thud. It seemed as though a large animal had jumped out from a nearby tree. I was aware that leopards frequently visited the IIT campus from the nearby Borivali National Park. I quietly put my arms around Aashu's waist and started walking back slowly towards the main road.

14

I was thrilled to have completed the first two years at IIT without a single 'summer'. 'Summer' at IIT meant the opportunity to repeat a subject one had failed in during the semester. I could see the possibility of completing the remaining two years with a similar record and then living with Aashu forever. Ramky had big ambitions of going to the US for higher studies and then pursuing a career there. My ambitions started and ended with Aashu. I could not possibly incur fate's wrath by asking for more. Fate had made the point ten zeros six nine probability come true for me already.

"Aashu, we should go outside Bombay somewhere this Durga *puja*. And spend some good time together." I suggested to her as she lay on my broad chest while I tried to read a book.

"Where do you want to go?" Aashu too seemed interested.

"I have never been to Khandala. What do you think of it?"

Khandala was one of the small cosy hill stations very near Bombay, on the Western Ghats.

"Good choice, Jeetu! I shall make the travel and hotel reservations soon. Just you and me?"

"No, I will have my father come with us too. He can evaluate his future daughter-in-law!"

Aashu smiled. Maybe at my humour but also probably at the thought of becoming my father's daughter-in-law.

We could not get a confirmed seat on the train to Khandala from Kalyan. But we still decided to go. I felt a bit sorry seeing Aashu stand for a couple of hours of the journey. I tried to support her as much as possible and stood behind her all the way with one arm around her slender waist and the other holding a pillar in the train. She let herself rest a bit on my well-built body. I liked the feeling of her body against mine. And I think she understood that from the slight bulge in my jeans.

We checked into a quaint-looking hotel hidden behind large trees at the end of a pebbled street. Our room was quite neat and had a window overlooking a verdant valley below. Khandala looks wrapped in green paper during most months of the year, especially during monsoons. This year the rains had continued for a bit longer than usual.

It was already 4 in the evening. I wanted the next few hours to run by quickly so that I could spend some intimate moments with her later that night.

"Aashu, let's go out for an early dinner tonight?"

She was happy to get out of the hotel. We took an umbrella from the hotel reception and started to walk towards the main street. It was drizzling slightly and I opened the umbrella. Aashu held herself tightly against me. I felt it was my duty to protect her from every drop of rain and I held her closely.

We had hardly walked for half an hour when I saw a familiar looking face among a group of boys and girls standing near a bus stand.

"Hi Jeetu!! What are you doing here?" A tall pretty girl shouted at me as soon as she saw us.

"Nirupama? Is that you? What a surprise!" She had grown into a ravishing girl with a very impressive personality. Her skin was slightly tanned and blemish-free. She was wearing a white shirt and jeans.

We quickly did the introductions for Aashu and others in her group. They were from her college in Bangalore where she was studying engineering.

"Where are you guys headed towards?" I asked Nirupama.

"Oh, we are going to the base of a nearby hill and then will trek for a couple of hours to the top. There is an ancient temple there. We will camp there for the night and then come back in the morning. It is going to be so exciting! Why don't you guys join us? It will be so much fun. We have an extra camping kit with us because one of the girls in our group fell sick at the last moment. Come on! Aashu, you should tell Jeetu to come!" Nirupama was in high spirits indeed.

Aashu looked at me. She could see I was interested. I liked to do such outdoor stuff. She knew that.

"Jeetu, let's go! I will inform the hotel that we will return tomorrow morning."

That's why I loved Aashu so much.

15

Mountains and I have a very deep bonding. I used to sit for hours together watching the Dalma hills from the terrace of my house in Jamshedpur. Whenever any relative visited us in Jamshedpur, I would offer to take them to the Dalma hills. I have often told Aashu that there are only five Ps that I lived for: *pyaar* (love), *paisa* (money), power, pictures (movies), and *pahad* (mountains). She would laugh at my 5 Ps theory. But this was real and true. It was not like the Bo Lon's theory.

The sun was playing hide-and-seek with the clouds. The drizzle had stopped but the clouds still hovered. We reached the base and started the trek uphill. There were seven of us. Nirupama walked with me and Aashu. Nirupama too was aware of my fascination with the mountains. I was whistling the tune of an old romantic song. I could see both Aashu and Nirupama smile. The trek meandered through a dense forest area where the rays of the sun barely made it through the trees and hit the trail in the form of a slim ray of light. The birds had started to return home. Perhaps they felt strange among visitors like us so late in the day.

We soon reached a green meadow. It was heavenly. I ran through the meadow with my arms stretched outwards as though trying to capture the entire beauty of nature in me. On one side of the meadow was a small waterfall gushing with fresh water from the mountains. We rested near the waterfall for a few minutes and also drank some water from it. We then resumed our trek.

Some distance away from the meadow, when the sun was just about to set, we came across a steep rock formation. It was not very high but it was slippery from the rains. One side of the rocks had a deep fall into the valley. We were all very cautious. I was the first one to climb the rocks. I then held out my hand to help others. Nirupama immediately reached out to grab my hands and then climbed up the rocks. I quickly glanced at Aashu who did not seem too happy with this. Soon, all of us were safely on top of the rocks and we proceeded on our final ascent towards the temple.

It was almost dark when we entered the flat ground where the temple was located. It was a small old temple made of stones. There was a small black stone inside the temple as a symbol of the idol. Some believed it to be God Shiva.

We quickly set up our tents and started a small fire to make some light dinner. It was one of the best dinners I have ever had, amid the mountains, staring at the sky filled with shining stars. One of Nirupama's friends broke into a Sufi song, which had a haunting feel to it in the eerie silence of the hills. Nirupama was quite at ease in the surroundings and was evident that she has been on similar treks before. As we sat there together after dinner, I could feel Nirupama looking at me. But whenever I turned to look at her, she looked in another direction.

There were four tents, and pairs were quickly made. Aashu and I were given the tent in the far corner of the ground. Nirupama was to sleep alone in one of the tents in the extreme corner of the ground. Aashu and I decide to retire early and went into our tents. It was very cosy and warm inside. The day was very tiring for Aashu and she quickly went into deep slumber.

I was a bit restless and could not sleep. Maybe it was due to the excitement of seeing Nirupama after all these years or maybe it was just the enticement of the lovely hills. I decided to take a walk and got out of the tent. I saw Nirupama sitting near the fire with a light blanket tightly wrapped around her. I walked towards her. She was a bit sad.

"What's wrong, Nirupama? Why are you looking so gloomy? Did you not like the dinner?" I tried to make her smile.

"Hey Jeetu. Looks like you too could not sleep. No nothing, just some old memories. Come, sit beside me."

I went and sat beside her.

"Jeetu, you know, I have always thought about you. But after that incident, I could not muster the courage to talk to you. I thought you and I were very compatible. Look, even small things like our love for the outdoor, the mountains, and nature..."

I got a little uncomfortable.

"It's so cold. You will fall ill. Come, let me share this blanket with you." She quickly extended the blanket to get a large part of me inside it.

"Jeetu, I am sure you think of me too. I know it's difficult to forget your first love."

How did she know she was my first love?

"Are you truly happy with Aashu? She seems so different from you."

As she spoke these words, her right palm settled on my left palm. She looked at me. And she moved her face closer towards mine. There was a slight creak of dry grass from behind us. We both got a jolt when we saw Aashu walking towards us. I took my hand away from Nirupama's hand and Aashu noticed this. I hoped it didn't look as bad as it seemed.

"I woke up and could not find you in the tent, Jeetu. So, I came looking for you. Do you want to stay here or come back and sleep?"

"Yes, it's quite late. Let us go to sleep."

I tried to remain calm.

Inside the tent, it no longer seemed warm. The chillness was quite apparent. Aashu turned the other side and went to sleep. I tried to nudge her.

"Do you want to talk about anything, Aashu?" She didn't reply.

The next morning, we hardly spoke to each other. The trek downhill was quite awkward. It was difficult to decide who was more silent – the forests around us or Aashu and me. When we reached Khandala, Nirupama asked us to join them for lunch.

"You go. I want to rest in the hotel," said Aashu.

"Are you sure?" I asked.

"Yes."

I decide to go ahead with lunch. I had not finished my conversation with Nirupama.

Lunch was a simple but tasty chicken curry with rice.

"Do you like the food, Jeetu?" Nirupama asked softly, wanting to take off from where we had left last night.

After lunch, I took Nirupama out for a short walk.

"Look Nirupama, I think you are a lovely and very talented woman. Had I not found Aashu as my soulmate, I would have certainly wanted to explore our potential relationship. But I cannot live without Aashu. She may not love the outdoors as much as you do. She may not even be as ravishing as you are in looks. But for me, she is ALL that I want. As long as she is alive or I am alive, I will not think of anybody. So, please do not take this any forward."

Nirupama could barely hold her tears. I knew she was very vulnerable at that moment. I decided to walk back towards the hotel. Nirupama just held her hand out in one last effort to hold me back somehow. But I was longing to be in the arms of someone else and I increased my walking pace to reach Aashu at the earliest.

"Sir, she has already left," the manager at the reception informed me.

Aashu had decided to take an earlier train.

16

I went through the worst period of my life for the next six months. Aashu simply refused to meet me or talk to me. I sent her many letters apologising to her if I had hurt her feelings in any way. But Aashu had made up her mind to not talk to me. It was not going to be easy to change that.

I barely managed to pass the rest of my subjects in the third year. However, I was determined to not let a summer derail my plans to live together with Aashu forever.

"You should focus on your studies man," Ramky would admonish me.

"Of what use is all this Ramky if I cannot live with my Aashu? The only reason I am still here attending classes and taking my examinations is that I don't want Aashu to feel bad later that I had to prolong my stay at IIT because of her. That would make her sad and I cannot bear that. I will make sure I at least pass all my subjects, Ramky."

I started to sob hysterically. I was a strong man but I was also a man with strong emotions. If I saw an emotional scene in a movie, I would start crying, often to the embarrassment of Aashu and others who were watching the movie with me. I never dreamt that I would have to deal with an emotional scene in my own life.

I was not looking forward to the summer holidays. How would I spend the days and nights, tormented by Aashu's separation, and with no classes or examinations to divert my mind? This time, my mother had come with my father to the railway station to receive me. I forgot my pain when I saw her. I touched her feet and hugged her and started crying. My father too had tears in his eyes.

Within a couple of days, my mother realised that something was amiss.

"Jeetu, what's the matter? You are not your usual self." All mothers seem to possess a doctorate degree in psychology when it comes to reading the minds of their children.

"*Ma*, have you ever fallen in love?" I was grown up enough to have this conversation with her, I thought.

"What kind of a question is that? In our times, we fell in love with our husbands only. And I was and am still in love with your father."

How could anyone fall in love with my father, I wondered.

"Then you can appreciate my state. I am deeply in love with this girl, Aashu. Aashana Verma. She lives in Calcutta and is upset with me. She has not been talking to me for many months now. But I know that we cannot live without each other for long. I just don't know what to do."

My mother was a traditional woman but had adapted herself well to the changing times. She knew that our family would not accept a woman outside our caste. But she said what a woman who loved her son would say.

"Go to Calcutta tomorrow Jeetu. Find her and win her back."

I hugged my mother and those tears flowed again. This time, they were of joy and pride.

As I got ready to leave my house early next morning to catch a train to Calcutta, my mother put a small red velvet pouch in my hands. It had a pair of gold earrings that she had got from my grandmother after her wedding.

"Someone who can make my strong son cry in this way must be special. And she deserves nothing less than something special. God bless you."

I barely managed to catch train. I quickly took the seat by the window, as the train moved towards Calcutta. Aashu had told me about her house and life in Calcutta. Her *dadu* had a brick kiln in Calcutta, a family legacy from Aashu's grandfather. The brick kiln was in Uttarpara, about half an hour by train from the main Howrah station.

Aashu had studied in JDS, a co-education school in Calcutta. Her family lived in a small two-bedroom apartment near the Howrah station. Every morning, Aashu would go to school by a bus while her *dadu* would catch the local train and go to Uttarpara to oversee the operations of the brick kiln. Aashu had no siblings. She was the lifeline of the family and was very close to her parents.

After Aashu moved to Bombay, her parents decided to move to Uttarpara where they had a small cottage near the brick kiln fields. There were many other brick kilns in the vicinity, some of them belonged to distant relatives of Aashu.

Aashu would often go to Uttarpara in the weekends while she was studying. She loved the company of her cousins. But her prime motivation for the weekend trips was the lovely fish curry and rice prepared at the kitchen run by the local staff of the brick kiln. The fish was often caught in the rivulet flowing along the cottage where Aashu's parents lived. This rivulet was connected to the Ganges river and the water was clean, with a daily ebb and tide period.

I took the local train to Bali, a station before Uttarpara, famous for its temple on the river banks. I went to a local stationery shop there and bought a bright red marker pen and a long sheet of white cardboard paper. From there, I went to the river banks, or *ghat* as it was called. I hired a local fisherman with a small boat, paid him the full money in advance, and gave him the directions to Aashu's brick kiln and cottage. Luckily, the fisherman was very familiar with the network of small rivulets in Uttarpara and he agreed to take me there willingly.

As we neared the cottage, I stood up and unfolded the sheet of paper. I had written on it in big bold letters – *Aashu, I can't say 'sorry' as there is no thank you or sorry between us. But please forgive me.*

I asked the fisherman to hold the boat steady in front of Aashu's cottage while I stood there in the afternoon sun with the white sheet stretched out.

Aashu's mother had stepped out of the cottage to do some washing. She saw me and then quickly rushed inside to call Aashu.

Aashu came out wearing a pristine white *salwar kurta,* her hair spread out. She had no make-up on her face and looked purer than the Ganges itself. Her lips quivered when she saw me and her tear glands could no longer hold the tears. She started crying. I jumped out of the boat onto the flight of stairs leading to her cottage and quickly ran up the stairs.

I had not planned the next step I took. I took the earrings my mother had given for Aashu and placed them in her hands. I put my other hand on her head, and said, "I will never make you unhappy again."

17

Aashu stood like a sculptured rock statue. She looked at me straight in the eyes. Her eyes were speaking out loud. I could hear a musical mix of love, anger, relief and joy.

"Jeetu, how can you suddenly show up like this and expect me to forgive you?"

"You are my soulmate, Aashu. We have no right to go against fate's plans for us. I love you like no one will in all your rebirths as a human being. I want to spend all of this life and the next lives with you. I will start running marathons, we can keep running together for the rest of our lives."

I could see the smile trying to peep out through her slightly parted and still trembling lips. She could no longer hold herself back and she hugged me tight. The fisherman on the boat seemed a bit embarrassed and I waved to him to go back.

"Jeetu, the three most important things in a relationship are trust, faithfulness and truth. If you can make theories, so can I! This is my TFT theory. Do you promise that for the rest of your life you will abide by this theory? I will also make the same promise to you."

If only she knew that I had already passed the TFT exam with flying colours! But this was not the time or place to explain all that.

"Yes, Aashu, I promise."

"I promise too." She said in the voice of a child.

She asked me to come inside their cottage. It was a small 3-bedroom cottage; one of the rooms was used by Aashu's *dadu* as the office. We entered through the back door and went into one of the rooms which also served as the living room during the day time. From this room, I could see a wooden door in the front, leading to a small garden enclosed by barbed wires. Beyond the garden was the brick field in which stacks of bricks were piled up neatly. And in the centre was a tall menacing iron chimney. The chimney was rusted in many places and was spewing obnoxious black smoke into the air.

"Hello Jeetu. We meet again." Aashu's *dadu* entered the room.

I went and touched his feet and he blessed me. Aashu told me later that he had been very impressed with this gesture.

Shortly afterwards, Aashu's mother, who in her youth must have been even more beautiful and graceful than Aashu, entered the room wearing a simple light coloured *sari*. She was carrying a tray containing at least three varieties of delectable sweets, some biscuits, and coconut water. I loved coconut water; I had read somewhere that it had the same chemical composition as our blood. I needed more blood in my body now after being drained of it over the past six months.

We sat there for a little while making small talk. Then *dadu* asked Aashu to show me around the place.

"But don't go too far."

Aashu nodded. She understood that her *dadu* meant not to go towards the houses of her cousins and other family members. An unknown boy walking with Aashu was not the kind of gossip that *dadu* or Aashu wanted.

Aashu took me around her own family's brick field. She explained how the raw material clay was procured from the rivulet and small ponds on their land and then tempered, moulded and dried before being fired in a furnace for days to turn it into hard bricks. It was a fascinating process and I was amazed to see Aashu's knowledge about it. She may have been studying economics in Bombay but her *dadu* had already taught her the real economics of daily life.

I saw many workers in the nearby mud huts. There were children with hardly any clothes running around and playing with abandon. You don't need to be rich to be happy – to be happy, you need to think happy.

After a couple of hours of walking around, we went back to the cottage and had some more coconut water. Aashu seemed to be normal again. In fact, she was better than normal. She was more assured and happier now. She was like the children playing outside, full of happy thoughts.

I was thrilled with her happy suggestion.

"Let's take our boat and go down the rivulet a little distance. I want to show you something." Aashu whispered into my ears.

The family had a small boat tied to the stairs near the rivulet, hidden behind some tall plants. In my excitement earlier, I had not noticed this boat. We both climbed onto the boat and started rowing it slowly with two wooden oars. Just about hundred metres down the rivulet, Aashu stopped rowing. She pointed to a nest on a nearby tree. At first, I could hardly see anything but after straining a bit I saw the marvellous sight. A beautiful hummingbird was building a small nest high up in the tree with some cotton fluff and soft plant parts.

"It has been building its nest for the past 5-6 days. It will complete it any moment now. Jeetu, this is a female hummingbird making a nest for her children."

"Where's the father hummingbird then?" I asked inquisitively.

"A female hummingbird does not let the male hummingbird come near its nest because of the bright colours of the male. The bright colours attract predators and this is not good for her children."

I should have guessed by now what was coming next.

"Jeetu, if you continue to remain very colourful and attractive to others, then my nest is under threat. I hope you understand that."

I looked at her. I was sure I wanted to build a nest and live in it with Aashu all my life. I had been thinking about this on the train journey from Jamshedpur. I had to do it now.

"Aashu, let's build a nest together. I will never make myself attractive to anybody or ever be attracted to anyone else. I want to marry you and live with you forever. Will you marry me?" By now, I was kneeling on the boat.

There was a slight wave in the rivulet and the boat tilted a bit making Aashu lose her balance slightly. She started to fall down but I caught her with my strong arms. We were now both kneeling in front of each other and our eyes were talking a million words to each other. And then her mouth said that one word, "Yes!"

I embraced her tightly in my arms. We stayed like that for at least 10 minutes and then we decided to go back to the cottage and share the news with Aashu's parents. As we rowed the boat back home, we both looked up and saw the hummingbird comfortably ensconced in the nest which was now complete.

18

We were both back in Bombay for our crucial final year. Aashu's parents were aware of our intentions now and my mother too knew. For all this strictness on most things, my father had a relatively liberal view on such matters. Maybe this was his way of showing his dissent against the traditional style and values of *baba*. Or maybe exposure to education and city life had made him more accepting.

My mother took just a couple of days to get my father to agree to our relationship. I remember my mother telling me later about my father's final statement.

"Look, I am okay with this. If it makes Jeetu and you happy, I am okay. After all, birth, marriage and death are the only three events that are preordained. Who am I to come in the way of that? The only one man who can come in way is Jeetu's *baba*. And I cannot take any responsibility for that."

I knew that *baba* would be a very tough nut to crack. I was already feeling a bit guilty for not having met *baba* for more than two years now. I was sure that the news of Aashu would have reached him by now.

His intelligence network was far superior to that of the Government of India.

A couple of weeks later, I was woken up by a junior at the hostel.

"Jeetu, get up. There is an urgent telephone call for you downstairs."

We had a small telephone booth near the 'mess'. We dreaded the calls from our homes. Usually, the news was not good.

"Jeetu, I have very bad news. *Baba* has been diagnosed with early stage cancer of the pancreas. The doctor has suggested that we take him to Bombay immediately for treatment." My mother sounded despondent.

"Don't worry, *ma*. I will try and take care of everything. Just call me again with the travel details and I will make the hospital bookings here. It will all be okay. *Baba* is a tiger killer. Cancer cannot kill him."

We got *baba* admitted to the Tata Cancer Hospital. The doctors suggested an immediate and intense dose of chemotherapy. *Baba* was against it.

"*Baba*, I have always listened to you, haven't I? Please for once listen to me?" I begged. *Baba* saw the tears in my eyes. There was no way he could turn down his favourite grandchild.

My father could not come with *baba* to Bombay due to his own ill health and work pressures. So *chachu* and *ma* had brought *baba* on a commercial Air India flight from Calcutta to Bombay.

The initial treatment period for chemotherapy was two weeks. During the day, I had classes and could not come to the hospital. So, *ma* and *chachu* stayed at the hospital for the whole day. One did the running around, while the other attended to *baba*. For two nights, *chachu* tried to stay over at night too while *ma* went to take rest in a nearby hotel. By the third morning, *chachu* was so fatigued that he just could not keep his eyes open. We knew this couldn't continue for two weeks.

My campus was too far away and I would spend at least an hour travelling each way. I shared my frustration with Aashu over the phone.

"Jeetu, I will be more than happy to attend to *baba* during the nights. My hostel is just 10 minutes away from the hospital and anyway I don't need sleep much at night as you know."

Aashu had a habit of taking a 20-minute nap during the afternoon and this strangely helped her be fresh after just 4-5 hours of sleep at night.

"But I don't know if *baba* will agree. He may get angrier and even stop his treatment."

I was not sure about this idea.

"Let's not tell him then. Can't you can just say that you have hired a nurse or something?"

Yes, that could work, I thought.

So, *baba* had a nurse called Shalu from the third night to attend to him. He was a little fussy in the beginning but then settled down quickly. Aashu was an angel for our family. She would talk to *baba* in Hindi and tell him fascinating stories of gods and kings. She would wash the saliva from his mouth and press his feet. She would clean and bandage his bed sores and sometimes even feed him at the middle of the night.

Baba actually started looking forward to the night time so that he could meet Shalu.

At the end of two weeks, there was a definite improvement in *baba's* health and the doctors were happy to release him on the condition that he would have to come for a check-up every three months.

Aashu and I went to see him together in the hospital on the morning of his release. *Ma* and *chachu* were busy getting the formalities completed for *baba's* discharge.

"*Baba*, I will miss you," Aashu said in earnest.

"No, you will not Shalu. Or shall I say Aashu?" *baba* replied.

We were both shocked and looked at each other.

"Jeetu, your *baba* has judged a thousand cases in the village as the local chief justice. I can read faces. There can be no girl in the city of Bombay who can take care of me with such love and dedication other than someone who was madly in love with someone I loved too. Jeetu, you are lucky to have Aashu. And I am happy to bless this relationship. And let me see who in this world has the strength to oppose my decision." *Baba* may have been weak after chemotherapy but his voice could still roar.

Aashu and I touched his feet and smiled at each other. There was no stopping destiny now.

19

We both decided not to pursue further studies. We had obtained solid education from reputed colleges. We wanted life to give us further education. We were ready to embrace life together.

Being a civil engineer, I decided to join a good engineering and construction company. There was L&T at the very top and then there were many others in the running for the second and third place. I knew I could have a stable long-term career with L&T. But I also knew I was not cut out for that. I wanted to join a company that was currently lower in ranks but had the aspirations to climb to the top.

The placement advisor at IIT asked me to consider Synfra Group. I had heard of the company. It was a Delhi-based upcoming corporate group with interests in construction and infrastructure. I did some research on the company and set up an appointment with its Managing Director, Jasraj Sinha, in Delhi.

As I walked into the three-storeyed glass façade building in Vasant Kunj, I felt a good vibe. I could see smiling faces all around. Happy people at the workplace is a good sign. I have never seen my father happy when he was going to work or returning from work. Work for him was only a way to earn money so that he and his family could survive in this world. I had promised to myself that I would never do such a job in my life where I didn't feel alive and happy every day.

"Sir, Jeetendra Singh is here to see you." The receptionist informed Jasraj Sinha.

I walked into a spacious room on the topmost floor of the building. The room opened into a very large balcony, which had a carpet of artificial grass, bordered with bright real flowers in red coloured pots. Jasraj Sinha was in the balcony talking to somebody on his mobile phone.

I sat down in one of the sofas in the corner of the room. The room was as big as my entire house in Jamshedpur. After I moved to Bombay, I quickly learnt that to be successful in life, one needs to have a big house, a big car, a big office, a big designation, and a big ego. The more ambitious ones also have a fancy degree and a pretty trophy wife. Jasraj probably had it all. But did he have a big heart was what I was concerned about.

"Ramakant, you have worked in our company for 17 years. Your daughter's wedding is like my sister's wedding. You can surely have a loan of 5 lakh rupees from the company and you don't need to pay any interest on it. And you can repay it whenever you are comfortable." I overheard Jasraj speaking on the phone.

The man seems to have a big heart, I thought.

Jasraj finished his conversation and entered the room shortly. He was about my age. And was very tall and handsome. His jet black hair was combed backwards and his sharp features resembled that of a movie star in my growing years at school. His skin was glowing and he had the confidence of a champion. He wore a black suit that fit him perfectly.

Jasraj's father had started the company almost 25 years ago and had built a good reputation. He was very happy when Jasraj joined him after completing his MBA from the London Business School.

"Good morning, sir," I greeted him with a smile.

"Call me Jasraj. And what do I call you? Jeetendra is too long a name, my friend!"

I didn't know if this was a trap to see how I responded or simply his nature.

I trust people. And treat their questions as simple questions, not traps. Other than the questions of my father, of course!

"Please call me Jeetu if you like, sir."

"No sir and all. I hate that word. Seems so much like an English legacy."

I had read somewhere that a candidate has just the first 20 seconds to make an impression on the interviewer. Jasraj had made more than an impression on the candidate in the first 20 seconds. The rest of the conversation was a pleasant formality and we soon shook hands.

"Welcome aboard, Jeetu. I am looking forward to working with you."

Aashu was thrilled on hearing about my job offer. She had waited for one month before confirming the employment choices she had. Aashu was a smart combination of a charming personality and intelligence, and hence had many offers during her campus interviews. She had shortlisted a multinational bank in Bombay and a real estate developer in Delhi. She hoped that I would find a job either in Bombay or Delhi.

Aashu confirmed her offer with the GLD Group the very next day. GLD was a large real estate development company based in Delhi. The promoter was an architect by the name Karan Grover. Initially, the company was known as Grover Land Developers but the name was changed to GLD Group after Karan Grover's daughter, Anu Grover, joined the group as a director.

Aashu and I decided not to take a break after graduation. We both flew together to Delhi to join work. We had a tough time finding a place to live in but finally found two rooms as 'paying guests' in separate floors of the same building in Vasant Kunj. It was a convenient location for us. The market was nearby, the autorickshaw stand was just in front of our building, and our offices were not too far either.

"Nothing is far Aashu, except you and me." I pulled her leg.

"Just wait for six months, my dear." She smiled impishly.

20

Aashu's parents came to Jamshedpur the following month to visit my parents. Arranging the marriages of their children was our parents' right and we wanted them to enjoy this right fully.

Dadu was a reasonable and practical man. He managed thousands of workers at the brick kiln every year and understood human emotions well, perhaps better than my father. My father was more methodical and logical in his approach than *dadu*. Aashu and I kept our fingers crossed, hoping that everything would be settled amicably between them.

"Singh *saab*, you know we are a small and happy family. I have given the best of upbringing to my daughter, and I am sure you will treat her as your daughter too," *dadu* said emotionally.

"Verma *ji*, daughters are daughters, and nobody can take their place. Aashu will remain a respected daughter-in-law in our family," my father said logically.

"Singh *saab*, I want the wedding to take place in Calcutta where all our friends are. It's not too far from Jamshedpur. And I will have the best of sweet curd and *rosogollas* prepared."

"Verma *ji*, I will have a lot of my friends and families coming from Jamshedpur, as well as from my village near Dhanbad. As you know, the trains to Calcutta are not reliable or they run at very odd hours. And the roads to Calcutta are pathetic too. In my opinion, Ranchi will be the most optimal point for people to travel from Jamshedpur and Dhanbad, as well as from Calcutta. I have a friend living in America who owns a large bungalow in Ranchi and he would be happy to make that available for the ceremony."

So, Ranchi was finalised as our wedding venue. I was partly happy because the weather in Ranchi was much better than that in Jamshedpur or Calcutta.

Aashu and her family arrived in Ranchi a week before the wedding. They had taken care of everything to the last detail – tent, lighting, food, drinks, entertainment, transport, hotel arrangements, priest, and so many other things. Aashu would normally have done most of the work herself but this time she was exempted. She kept herself busy by going to the spa, the salon, and the local gym. She also shopped for the best of *saris* and jewellery. *Dadu* had just one daughter and he wanted to make sure she was married off in style.

I arrived in Ranchi just a day before the wedding. My family came in buses hired from Jamshedpur and Dhanbad. My younger cousins had great fun on the way, dancing merrily to the latest Bollywood songs. Weddings are great party places for the young and old. The older ones enjoyed the vast choice of special liquors my father had arranged. As I have always said, alcohol is a distant cousin of human beings. So, how could they be missing from such an important event?

On the evening of our wedding day, I was wearing a light blue suit and a tie. And as was the tradition in our family, I had to wear a special turban and carry a sword by my side. *Baba* was also there along with Bhola and others from his village. They were all carrying guns with them. *Baba* had a silver pistol tucked in a small pouch around his waist. I prayed to God that Aashu would not notice these arms and ammunition that were about to proceed towards the venue.

I had decided to go with the *baraat* in a car, and not on a horse as was the tradition. *Baba* was not happy about this but he eventually relented. There were about 500 people in the *baraat* and we had to cover about a kilometre by road to reach the venue. I had never seen such wild dancing by everyone in the family, including the women.

Chachu and *choti chachi* were gyrating to some snake songs. A cousin was doing the moon walk steps. But the best dance was that of Bhola with my father. They were dancing in sync to the steps of an old movie song of Dilip Kumar. But the hand and leg movements were more that of Amitabh Bachchan. Maybe this was my father's gift to me.

And then the band started playing a famous Amitabh Bachchan song. I couldn't resist any more. I got out of the car, much to my mother's disappointment, and joined the dance party. With a sword in one hand, I was enacting all the dance steps of Amitabh Bachchan that I remembered, hoping Aashu would catch a glimpse.

We reached the venue amid the usual fireworks and gun shots. Then we were garlanded by Aashu's family.

I went in and sat on the main stage like a king. My friends and families happily clicked photographs on their cameras from every angle. And then Aashu was escorted to the stage by her cousins. She sat on the chair next to me, looking no less than a queen in her red *ghagra choli*. The photographers from both families went berserk clicking pictures and we felt like royalty, allowing the loyal subjects to capture these moments for the sake of memory. Amid all the excitement, I felt someone pinching me on my waist from under the armrest of my chair. It was Aashu. She was smiling. She was happy in the knowledge that in the next hour or so we would be formally recognised as husband and wife in the eyes of society and law. She was happy in the thought that fate would be smiling at us, content that its plans had worked perfectly for us so far.

I decided to break tradition again while garlanding Aashu. I placed the garlands quickly around her neck and then guided her hands so that she could place the garlands around my neck, before my family could make it difficult for us. We then proceeded towards the area where the rest of the rituals were to be performed. On the way, I noticed Neha *didi*, her husband, and their son sitting in a dark corner of the garden. Good of them to have come, I thought.

The priest was chanting the hymns and *mantras*. Our immediate families were standing around a partially-open enclosure. Within the enclosure was a neatly arranged pile of wood, with red bricks all around. I tried to see if those bricks were from Aashu's brick kiln but I then heard the priest shout. "Sir, please start your seven rounds around the sacred fire."

After every round, Aashu was supposed to touch a grinding stone with her toes and not move forward till I lifted her toe and requested her to continue. This was part of the tradition. Probably to demonstrate that the husband was willing to bow down and pamper his wife during the various stages of life. I thought this was just a symbolic tradition. But Aashu took it very seriously. She actually refused to lift her toe easily and I had to gather all my strength to lift it and continue with the proceedings. This happened after every round. Aashu could not hide the smile beneath the thin layer of cloth covering her head and face.

Aashu then sat on the ground while I put orange vermilion on her forehead as the final act of solemnising the marriage. I looked down at her while smearing the vermilion and noticed small but familiar letters written on the ground with vermilion. It said 'TFT'.

21

Jasraj could not make it to my wedding as he had some important family function. When I returned to office after the wedding, he called me to his office.

"Jeetu, congratulations! May you and your wife live happily ever after! Enjoy the journey of life my friend, and to do that, this will come handy." He handed me a set of keys. "These are the keys to your new Hyundai Accent car kept in the parking outside."

I had seen a shining blue Accent outside the office and had wondered who the proud owner could be.

"This is great, Jasraj. Thanks a lot!" I shouted with joy and gratitude.

Jasraj was an astute businessman. He knew where to make his investments. He was investing in me. In the past 6-7 months, he had seen some potential in me. And he had made me in charge of the New Businesses department too.

Over the next couple of years, I worked very hard. In the last few years, Jasraj had grown the business in the infrastructure sector. He believed India needed world-class roads for the economy to prosper and he was going to make Synfra the leading road builder in the country. I supported his strategy fully but I also pushed Synfra's team to take up more building construction works. I believed there was a huge shortage of housing in India and somebody had to construct those houses. I went to China and brought the latest cost-effective technologies for quick construction in India.

Synfra's revenues started to grow rapidly. We split the business into the infrastructure and buildings verticals. I then added the services verticals. We acquired two mid-sized companies in the areas of security services and facility management services. Synfra was emerging as a leading integrated asset delivery and operations management company in the country. I often got calls from executive search firms tempting me with splendid opportunities within and outside India. But Synfra was not just a job for me. And Jasraj was not just a boss. Synfra was family and Jasraj was like the brother that I never had.

Jasraj and I loved travelling together. He would take me to the most expensive restaurants for the best food and wine.

I once asked him, "Jasraj, you spend more than a million rupees every year in just eating out – imagine the number of stomachs you could feed with that kind of money!"

"You are right, Jeetu. But I look at it in another way. Eating out makes me happy, it makes me feel inspired and motivated. And then I can do better at work and create more job opportunities. And that way, feed many many more families."

I could not argue with that logic.

We had to go to London for closing a very large deal for a joint venture with a European company that would help grow our infrastructure business as well as bring a lot of debt funding. This deal was a game-changer. Jasraj asked the CFO and me to come with him to London.

On the flight, I tried to instill in Jasraj belief in God. He was not much of a believer.

"Jasraj, by my mathematical logic, I think you should turn into a believer soon. There is a 50/50 probability of God being there or not being there. But in the event that he is there, it will serve you well to believe in him. In business parlance, this is called protecting your downside."

"Ha ha Jeetu! Well put! But tell me if God is actually there, will he want me to believe in him blindly? Or if he is within all of us, as you say sometimes, then will he not make me believe in him from within? Some say fear God and he will punish you if you don't believe in him. I say Jeetu, will God punish me for me to start believing in him or will he reward me for just believing in him?"

I was a bit confused in these matters and my engineering background did not help. We were taught not to accept anything at face value unless detailed and sustained proven observations established the hypothesis.

"But Jasraj, I believe in destiny. I met my wife because it was destiny. As our sages say, it's all pre-written for everybody."

"Exactly! If it is pre-written, then why do you need to pray? Why do you need to trouble God and make him go and change what he has written? Do you know he will have to do more than six billion edits for human beings alone every time he agreed to a request to change something that was destined and pre-written – just to keep the wheel of life rolling?"

I decided it was more enjoyable to watch the new American movies on the screen in front of my seat than discuss philosophy with Jasraj.

I soon felt very sleepy and tired and went into a deep slumber.

I got up after a couple of hours. We were still flying over the ocean. I felt different though. For the first time in my life, I remembered the dream I had in my sleep. I could never remember any dream in the past. I was not even sure if I had had any dreams. Maybe my dreams were all for Aashu. And I saw those dreams during day time too.

I had dreamt that the office of the company we were to form a joint venture with was closed and locked. There were angry investors protesting and shouting in front of the office. I could not remember any more than this.

I told this to Jasraj who was still watching an inflight Bollywood movie. He first laughed out aloud but then had a slightly concerned look on his face. His brain quickly did the math and planned what to do in the event this did happen. He did not speak much for the rest of the flight.

During the negotiations in the boardroom with the London company, Jasraj insisted on equity funding and not debt funding from the company. This was completely different from what we had discussed and agreed upon earlier but Jasraj stood his ground and firmly said, "Either this or no deal, gentlemen." After a few hours of internal deliberations, the company finally agreed to this and we signed the deal. We uncorked a bottle of champagne to celebrate the occasion.

A week after we returned to India, the equity funds from the European company had reached Synfra's bank account. The funds were now available to be used for growing the Indian business, as per the directions and business plans approved by Synfra's board, a majority of which was controlled by Jasraj's family.

A couple of weeks later, we saw a news on TV about the European company being involved in a major accounting fraud. This had led to bankruptcy of the company. The TV cameras zoomed in on the company's office building, which was locked. There were many angry shareholders shouting outside the building.

It sent shivers down my spine. How could this happen? Was it just a coincidence or was there more to it? My engineering mind dismissed any more debate on the subject.

Jasraj was in the happiest of moods. He had the funds, and he knew, as per the agreement, he was under no obligation to return it immediately. If he had taken the funds as debt, he would have been under tremendous pressure to return it, bear the transaction costs, and find alternative sources of funding.

"Jeetu, I believe in you and your dreams. Dream big, my friend, and we shall build a billion-dollar company together soon."

Jasraj and I became very close after this incident. I kept climbing the corporate ladders with unprecedented velocity.

22

We had taken a 4-bedroom apartment in Gurgaon, an upcoming suburb of Delhi. We did not mind the long drive from home to our offices. Gurgaon was home to a lot of malls; the malls had multiplexes that screened the movies Aashu and I so loved so much. And when people watch movies, they like to eat good food. So naturally, several interesting restaurants came up in Gurgaon. The airport was also quite near. This was convenient as both Aashu and I had to travel often.

Aashu was very happy at GLD Group. She became happier when it was announced that GLD would be shifting its head office to a commercial building in Gurgaon, only 10 minutes from where we lived. We now had more time for each other, more time to talk, and more time to make love and, hopefully, make a baby.

Aashu was doing very well at GLD. She had joined the finance team, and soon moved to the marketing and sales department. The people who bring in the *moolah* in any business are the ones who get the most respect and the most promotions. The real estate market was doing well. Many of GLD's projects were in Gurgaon, which was a hot destination. Projects were sold even before they were launched. The Gurgaon real estate market was emerging as the new bank for the black money of North India.

Karan Grover was a kind and generous promoter. He gave a lot of flexibility to Aashu to work from home; she had flexible hours and could go on holidays any time. All this helped a lot in the early years of marriage and in my professional commitments at Synfra. Aashu had a natural flair for marketing. She was the obvious choice to take decisions on marketing and media campaigns. Her job was very fulfilling. Till Anu Grover came.

Anu was Karan's younger daughter. Anu's elder brother was not interested in business. He had chosen academics as his career in the US. Anu had an MBA from Stanford. She had worked with the Hilton group in Europe as a development manager. I had met her briefly during a business meeting I had gone with Jasraj. We had tried to secure a construction contract from GLD.

Anu was of medium height and was very cute with petite features. Her hair was smooth and straight. Her skin was flawless and her smile very charming. But beneath the graceful façade lay a very ambitious and ruthless personality. She knew what she wanted and knew how to get it.

One night, Aashu came back home late. She was very upset.

"What happened?" I asked her gently.

"That Anu! What does she think of herself? We were deciding the name of the new apartment complex project and I suggested 'Rose'. She burst out laughing in front of the whole group and told me to broaden my horizon beyond a traditional Indian woman from a village."

Aashu was fuming.

"Yes, I am happy to be a traditional Indian woman, even though I am not from a village. What would she have done if she were not Karan Grover's daughter? She would have probably not got a job even in a local bank in *baba's* village."

I wanted her to let it all out.

"Do you know what they say about her in office? At Hilton, in London, she had fallen in love with a Sri Lankan guy who was her colleague. But the guy was in love with a British woman working in the same office. Anu reported to her superiors that she was very uncomfortable working with the guy. He was then transferred back to Sri Lanka. But the British woman did not want to shift. Anu had gloated to her close friends later that if the guy could not be hers, then he could not be anybody else's too."

"Forget her, Aashu. Let us take a day off tomorrow and watch the latest Shahrukh Khan movie." Aashu was a Shahrukh fan and our rare fights was over who was better – Shahrukh or Amitabh.

We were the only couple that we were aware of who saw a 10 a.m. show at the multiplex. We found that to be the most convenient. There was no chitter-chatter from the people sitting next to you or behind you. Parking was easy in the mall. And we would be out in time for lunch.

This time we were the only people in the multiplex. I teased Aashu about Shahrukh's dwindling popularity. I didn't know if she had become upset with that but she looked sullen. To make her happy, I danced in front of the screen to the most popular song in the movie.

She was happy after the movie. We had had a heavy breakfast. So, we decided to go back home and have lunch. I have never been much of a cook but there was a larger conspiracy by my hormones that day. I wanted to please Aashu that day so that we would be in the right frame of mind to make a baby. We had been planning for the right moment for the past month or so. Today was the day, and my hormones knew it.

"Let me cook for you today, dear," I proudly proclaimed.

"What? Don't be mad. What are you going to cook? I am in no mood for Maggi now."

"I will cook healthy brown rice and red beans and sausage mixed curry. How does that sound?"

'It sounds delicious. Let's see if it tastes delicious too."

I told her to go to her room and listen to some music while I went to the kitchen and got ready for the challenge.

With the readymade can of red beans and cut sausages and a rice cooker gifted by *dadu*, I was on a roll. Within an hour, the food was ready. I placed small portions of the curry and rice on a plate and took it on a tray to her room.

Her face lit up when she saw me bringing the food. I waited with bated breath for her to taste the food.

She did and then looked up and said, "I am really impressed. From now on, every Sunday, you shall have this opportunity."

We both laughed. And so did my hormones.

After lunch, we watched a bit of TV and then came back to our room. I brushed my teeth and gargled my mouth with the most expensive mouthwash. She was lying on the bed in a T-shirt and denim shorts. Her legs were clean shaven and looked as shapely as they were on the day I ran behind her with glucose water. Through her T-shirt, I could see the silhouette of her milky white bosom. I lay down beside her, turned her around, and spooned her with my arms closely encircling her curvy waist. I then whispered into her ears softly from behind, "Let's make a baby, darling."

She didn't say a word. She just turned around and gently kissed me on the lips.

Our love was special that day. Just like it had been on our honeymoon.

23

After our wedding in Ranchi, we had just four days to spare for our honeymoon. We had debated many options for honeymoon in the month before our wedding.

"I wanted to go to Switzerland, Aashu."

"So that we can dance in the Alps? Ha ha!" Aashu could never stop laughing at my obsession with the movies.

"What about Agra and Taj Mahal? That will be romantic," Aashu had suggested.

"What is romantic about going to someone's graveyard?" I knew I was being unreasonable. The Taj Mahal was indeed a marvel of the world. Perhaps I felt envious of Shah Jahan for having made such a monument for his lover.

"Aashu, my love, you are like my goddess. Hence, there can be no other land more befitting for our honeymoon than the land of the gods, Kerala!" I am sure the gods would not have appreciated this logic.

We were very tired after the wedding ceremonies and really looked forward to our trip to Kerala. On the flight to Kerala, Aashu caught up with the much needed sleep. I was too excited to get any sleep. Aashu and I knew each other so well but this trip was going to bring us closer. We had kissed passionately a few times before but Aashu was not comfortable in going beyond that before marriage.

We reached our resort in the backwaters near Cochin. Our villa was a spacious one overlooking the backwaters. There was a living room with comfortable sofas and a TV. The place was immaculately clean and well-maintained.

We quickly unpacked our bags and went out to have a sumptuous buffet lunch. I loved the simple tomato-based fish curry while Aashu feasted on the *appam* and vegetable stew. I had this habit of overeating at buffets. It is the middle-class mindset in me that wants to maximise the returns on every rupee spent. It is the genetic coding in me that wants to store as much food in me to overcome any potential drought situation later. Aashu teased me for this logic and asked me to factor in the medical costs due to overeating.

With all the food in my stomach, I could only think of catching a good afternoon nap. We went to our villa, pulled up the clean white and smooth blankets over us, and went to sleep. Neither of us had the libido or physical energy to think of anything else at that time. Our energies were fully occupied in digesting the heavy food we had just had.

Usually, when I sleep late in the afternoon, I feel very depressed upon waking and seeing the sun go down the horizon. Today, I felt great seeing the sun go down. It was a perfect setting with the red sky above us and the sky blue waters of the backwaters in front of us. The sky and the backwaters seemed to be merging in the horizon. It was a perfect union. And I could not but help fantasising about the perfect union with Aashu later that night.

We decided to hire a small boat to take us into the calm backwaters in the late evening. It was not too long ago that a similar boat ride had changed our lives, I thought.

It was a beautiful evening and we could see the backwaters all around and the trees on the sides. Sometimes an odd boat crossed us. We came across an underpass where some children were standing and staring at us, probably wondering why we were out on a boat so late in the day. Aashu and I sat close to each other. I tried to write words on her hand with my fingers. She loved it when I wrote on her hand or her back. I generally asked her to guess what I had written. Today, it was not difficult for her to guess.

"I love you." She had no hesitation in guessing what I had written.

While food was the last thing on my mind, I did want to have a light and early dinner that night. Tonight was going to be the night of fusion. Fusion of our taste buds too. I asked the boatman to make a simple home prepared meal of *appam* and fish curry for us. We sat like royalty while he laid out the table for us. It was one of the best meals I had ever had and it definitely was the best place I had ever eaten a meal. We could not thank the boatman enough. He had stirred the passions within us through the heavenly food. It was indeed food of the gods in the land of the gods.

On the way back, the boatman started to sing a local song. We could not understand a word of it but it did remind me of an Amitabh Bachchan movie in which he took a gondola ride in Venice with the beautiful heroine. That was the final aphrodisiac I needed.

We entered the room. We did not wait to brush our teeth or wash our mouths. We started to passionately kiss in the living room. Aashu hurriedly unbuttoned my shirt while I focussed more on her lips and tongue. We had no shame in taking out all our clothes in front of each other for the first time. In the dim and diffused light of a lamp kept in the corner of the living room, her body looked a work of art. Her face was very fair but the rest of her body, hidden from the sharp glares of the sun, was much fairer. Her curves were in the right places; she was shapelier than what I had imagined. She had red moles dotted along the contours of her body, which excited me tremendously, as I had only seen black moles in my life. And I understood why they say red is an exciting and passionate colour.

We collapsed on the nearby sofa, with me on top of her. She guided me with care and I gently entered her. The warm feeling of her body matched the warmth and love in her light brown eyes. She was holding me tight, not wanting to leave an iota of space between our bodies. Our souls may have waited for centuries for this union but we were in no hurry. I wanted to make sure the experience was the most pleasurable for her. I had not forgotten my promise of being selfless in making love to her. We climaxed together and hugged each other even more closely. I could feel her rapid heartbeats trying to convey a message to me that we shall always remain close, forever and ever.

24

I was mad at Ramky for not having come to our wedding. But he had gone to the US immediately after IIT to pursue a PhD in physics from MIT. Ramky was a topper in our class at IIT and had scholarship offers from almost all the top colleges in the US. He chose MIT because he believed he would be able to pursue his passion in physics and learn more about the universe.

Ramky often called me from the US, especially at odd morning hours in India.

"Jeeeeetuuu! What's happening, man? I really miss you, dude."

The American influence on his accent was getting stronger. The Indian influence of love for alcohol was also getting stronger. He would drink late in the night and then call me sometimes.

"This is an awesome place, Jeetu. I am having so much fun here. There is so much freedom to explore here…" He was in high spirits that day.

"Hope you are not exploring too much, Ramky! I don't think uncle and aunty in Machilipatnam would be too happy eating *sambhar* rice made by a *gori.*" I cut him short.

Ramky went on to finish his PhD in a record time of four years. He then got bored. Great minds like him need constant motivation. So, he decided to pursue an MBA from Harvard.

As was expected from Ramky, he topped his MBA class too and was picked up by a leading private equity company in the campus interview. He had to move to New York, which I thought was a good thing for him. He would be constantly challenged and motivated by the diversity and intricacies of New York City.

It had been a while since I last spoke to him. I heard that he was doing wonderfully well at the private equity company.

It was not often that I called Ramky. The cost of a call per minute from India was too much and Ramky discouraged me to call.

He would say, "Just give me a missed call, Jeetu. I have number identification on my phone. And I will call you back."

I now deploy this strategy with my driver who gives me a 'missed call'.

But today was special and I could not think of sharing this news with anyone else other than Ramky, after my parents and Aashu's parents.

"Ramky, too busy? Heard you are a big man now. But you will be happy to know you are going to become a big uncle now." I was on the speaker, with Aashu standing next to me.

"What? That's great news, Jeetu. You have done the greatest good for this universe! Where is Aashu?" He and Aashu shared a good relationship over the phone although they had never met in person.

"Hi Ramky. How are you?" said Aashu.

"Aashu! Congratulations! I am so thrilled. Hope the baby boy or girl will have both your brains and looks. The universe can't afford to have another Jeetu." And they both laughed heartily.

Aashu continued to work for the next seven months. She consciously tried to avoid any confrontation with Anu at work. Her office was very nearby and she often came back home in the afternoon to take rest for an hour or so.

Anu Grover was gradually taking full control over GLD. Karan Grover was happy to spend more time on the golf course and throw lavish parties at his palatial bungalow in Vasant Vihar. We were invited to one of these parties to celebrate GLD's signing of a large deal with a leading financial institution.

"I don't think I shall be able to go this party," Aashu said in a slightly tired voice. "But I think you should go. Otherwise Karan sir will not like it." She insisted.

"What will I do there without you, Aashu?"

"Don't worry. You will find people you know. And I am sure you will make some new friends."

The party was on a Saturday night. I decided to go straight from my office to the party. I reached by about 8 p.m. But parties in Delhi never really start before 9 p.m. I was greeted at the main gate by a manager and escorted to a living room which was larger than our 4-bedroom apartment. There were paintings of M. F. Hussain all over the living room. The huge glass chandelier on the ceiling covered almost a third of the living room area. I must add this to my 'big' list after becoming successful in life, I thought. One must also have a very big chandelier, I told myself.

There were a few other people, mostly young couples, who had arrived earlier than I. They were quickly gulping down glass after glass of expensive red wine. I could understand why they had arrived so early.

I sat alone in a corner sipping a glass of white wine.

"You like to be alone, don't you?" I heard a voice from behind me. I turned and saw Anu Grover standing there in a shiny black dress with a bold slit up to her thighs. She was wearing a necklace made of several large pieces of green emerald. It ended where her deep cleavage started. She was attractive, no doubt.

"Hi Anu. I am not sure if you know me. My name is Jeetendra. Most people know me as Jeetu. We had briefly met once at your office for a meeting with Synfra where I work. I am Aashu's husband."

"Oh yes, I do remember you, Jeetu. It's not every day that you come across a man with a personality like yours." She sat in front of me in the elaborate sofa.

"Thank you, Anu. So, how is work going? I hear your GLD is expanding in a big way." I tried to change the subject.

"My GLD? Ha ha! Nice way of putting it, Jeetu. In today's world, no one owns anything or anybody – it's all shared, isn't it?"

"Well, depends." I didn't know how to respond.

"Tell me, does anyone ever ask you about YOUR Aashu?" She stressed on 'your'.

"It's all a contractual world and relationships are also contractual. I am with GLD till the time the shareholders are happy with me. You are with Aashu till the time you are happy with her."

I wanted to tell her that I would be with Aashu for eternity. I was a bit upset with her remark. And she noticed that.

"Oh, I didn't mean it in any other way. So, how is Synfra doing? You guys are building one of our high-rise projects in Mumbai. How is that going? We should maybe go there together once to review the project?"

"Yes, why not? Just let me know when."

She then excused herself to mingle with the other guests. I saw Karan Grover enter the room then. I went up to him and introduced myself. I shook hands with him warmly. It was around 9.30 p.m. by then.

I thought of skipping dinner. I was gaining a lot of weight, especially around the belly.

"You are a true husband, Jeetu. Your tummy is growing at the same pace with which the baby is growing in my tummy!" Aashu teased me often.

I looked around to see if Anu was there so that I could say goodbye before leaving. I could not find her. Anu was not someone you could find easily. If she wants to, she will find you, I thought.

25

India was playing South Africa in a cricket test match in Cape Town. The stadium was filled with people. Tendulkar scored a smashing 169 runs and Azharuddin too scored a century.

I woke up in the morning and was surprised to remember the 'dream' again. I told this to Aashu. She knew about my earlier dream on the flight to London.

"The next test match is just a week away. Let us see if the Indian cricket team heroes will come anywhere near the scores in my dream. I will be thrilled if they do. But then I will also be scared of you," said Aashu.

We watched the test match on TV with a mix of excitement and trepidation. Tendulkar went on to score 169 runs and Azharuddin 115. India still lost the game to South Africa. The whole country was grieving and debating what had gone wrong with our cricket team. Aashu and I were curious to know what had gone wrong with the universal laws. How could this happen? Was I getting the so-called 'premonitions'? Or was it just coincidence?

"Jeetu, I think it's because you think so much. Your mind works out various calculations and probabilities, and then one of them turns out to be real. That's it."

"But why does the one scenario out of a theoretical infinite outcomes become true in the future? And that too it occurs in my dream, which I strangely happen to remember!" I exclaimed.

"Don't worry about it too much. Let's just celebrate Tendulkar's century," Aashu suggested. Like most of India, she was happy about Tendulkar's century than sad about India's loss.

We had no idea at that moment that our celebrations would continue the next day as well.

Early next morning, Aashu's water broke and she was admitted to the nearby hospital for a caesarean operation, as advised by her doctor earlier. She was taken to the operation theatre while I nervously waited outside. I called my parents and told them to take a flight to Delhi immediately.

Around noon, the nurse came out smiling, and said it was a boy. I was a father! It was a powerful feeling. Somebody depended on me, someone would look up to me for guidance, protection, affection. My thoughts immediately went out to my father. I had tears in my eyes.

Our boy was a healthy and happy baby. I could see him only from the glass panes of the area where there were at least 10 other new born babies. He was wrapped in a blanket with only his face showing. His eyes opened a bit and he had the same light brown eyes of Aashu. I thought he smiled at me. I made sure I observed and recorded every feature of his in my mind, just in case he got exchanged by mistake!

Aashu was brought back to the room in an hour. I went up to her and kissed her.

"Congratulations, my dear!"

"You too, Aashu!"

"Have you thought of a name for him?" Aashu asked me.

"No, but I don't want him to have a surname that represents my caste. Let us do one thing. You choose the first name and I will choose the second name. We will join it and that will be his full name!"

"My choice is Rahul." Not surprising, I thought, considering Aashu was a big Shahrukh Khan fan.

"My name for him is Vijay." Vijay was the reel name of Amitabh Bachchan in most of his movies.

"Then he is Rahul Vijay!" We both exclaimed, nearly in unison.

At home, Rahul Vijay was called Aarvee (RV). The letter 'A' was doubly lucky for me. The name 'Aashu' started with two As and so did 'Aarvee'.

My parents arrived the day we brought Aarvee home. They were excited beyond words. Becoming grandparents is like having done full justice to your journey of life. They spent most of their time around Aarvee. I was amazed to see my father take so much care of the baby. I felt a bit jealous too. One evening, while he was sitting alone in the balcony holding Aarvee in his laps, I went up to him.

"*Papa*, I am sorry for everything."

"Sorry for what, Jeetu?" He barely looked up.

"For being the son I would not have wanted to be a father of." I could not put it in any other way.

My father got up and placed his right hand on my head and ruffled my hair. He then said, "Son, becoming a father has made you wiser. But let me tell you, I was always proud of you. I just expected so much from you. Perhaps, I wanted you to fulfil your potential *and* my dreams, and make up for the skills and opportunities *I* never had. Don't make this mistake with your son."

Since then, my father and I shared a special bond and relationship.

26

Aashu had taken maternity leave for two months. She then returned to GLD and continued to work there for the next three years. Aashu's parents and my parents took turns visiting us and taking care of Aarvee. The economy was picking up and I was doing very well at Synfra.

"Aarvee will soon start going to school. I think one of us needs to have flexible work timings to take care of him," I proposed to Aashu.

"You are doing so well at Synfra. You should not disturb that. I am anyway quite fed up of this Anu Grover. I better resign from GLD soon before I slap her one day in front of everybody."

Aashu and Anu were clearly not getting along. I was not sure if it had something to do with Synfra's and my growing business relationship with GLD.

Aashu resigned from GLD the next week. She was given a farewell party in office; everyone but Anu attended the party. Anu excused herself to meet some politician.

I had come back from Karan Grover's party and told Aashu about my encounter with Anu. Aashu had warned me mockingly, “My handsome Jeetu, please be very careful of her. She will bewitch you with her seductive looks one day. And then eat you, devour you completely, and spit your mangled mess of mashed bones and muscles.” She had made Anu look like a complete witch. I briefly imagined Anu with dishevelled hair, long nails, and feet turned inwards, coming towards me with her tongue hanging out.

“Don’t worry, Aashu. As long as I wear my TFT protection band, no witch can do any harm to me.” I reminded her pompously.

“Hey there.” I heard a woman’s voice as I picked up the call from an unknown number a few days later after Karan Grover’s party.

“Sorry, who is this?”

“Someone you seem to have forgotten very quickly, Jeetu. Anu, Anu Grover, from GLD.”

“Oh hi! Sorry, I didn’t have your number Anu.” I apologised.

“I thought we were to go to Mumbai for our project review together?” She reminded me.

“Oh, again so sorry, Anu. I forgot to follow up on that.”

“You don’t need to say sorry to me Jeetu, ever. Okay?” She said in a soft voice.

No sorry, no thank you. I had made this pact with only one woman in my life, Aashu. Anu was not going to change that.

“Let’s meet in Mumbai next Tuesday.” I changed the subject quickly.

The Mumbai project was a high-rise residential apartment being developed by GLD. It was one of the tallest structures in Worli. It was a 50-storey building and the penthouses were worth several million dollars. The economy was getting better and real estate was always a favourite investment destination of the rich and famous. The demand for the project was strong but our construction speed was slow. Anu was not too happy about this.

Anu and I wore protective helmets and hard boots. We took the temporary elevator to go to the topmost floor of the building. The structural works were almost over now; the finishing and external work had to be started.

We took a tour of the top floor while the managers and supervisors followed us. I could see the sea from up there. It looked so still and tranquil. I remembered the several hours that Aashu and I sat on the rocks near the sea during the weekends when we were in college. I had never imagined that I would be seeing the same sea from such an elevation one day.

We walked to the edge of the open terrace. My manager cautioned me to not go any further. Anu moved a bit forward to see how small the world looked from that height. She wanted the world to be small in front of her.

As she neared the edge, Anu's feet got entangled in some loose rebars kept on the floor and she was about to fall down. I barely managed to grab her hands in time and prevented her from falling. I remembered Aashu falling on the boat in Uttarpara before I had proposed to her. I seemed to have a gift of protecting women from falling. But I could not protect women from falling in love if they desired so.

Anu looked at me longingly as she recovered. She did not let go of my hands for some time.

"Thank you, Jeetu. You probably saved my life. I am indebted to you now forever. May you have the power to take it away again if I hurt you any day!"

Anu liked to be dramatic. I was not even sure if she would have fallen off the building or landed on the protective net placed below the terrace.

That evening, we decided to have dinner in a newly opened 5-star hotel. Jasraj was also in town and he decided to join us. Anu did not look too happy about this and it was visible on her face.

"Anu, we are now one of the leading contractors for buildings works in the country. Why does GLD have to float a tender every time? Synfra and GLD can have a transparent arrangement whereby Synfra automatically manages all of GLD's projects. You will save a lot of management time and cost with this and you will also be assured of quality delivery." Jasraj was at his best as a salesman.

"Not a bad idea, Jasraj. I am impressed with Jeetu's knowledge and relationship management skills," said Anu. She briefly looked at me and winked. And then continued. "If he is nominated as the senior account manager dealing directly with GLD, then I am happy to do this deal."

Jasraj was thrilled at the prospect and immediately agreed. Later that night, after Anu had left, Jasraj told me over drinks at the bar, "Jeetu, you seem to have done some magic on Anu. Anu would never have done such a deal so easily. You have mellowed her down my friend. Tell me what is your secret, chief?"

"Come on, Jasraj! You know I can never go astray. But I was thinking that both of you actually make a great match." I smartly tried to throw the monkey off my shoulder.

"I have told you before, Jeetu. My love stars were never properly aligned for this life. The only girl I really liked and would have married never even knew I was in awe of her. Leave that, she probably didn't even know my name."

Jasraj had briefly mentioned once earlier about this girl in school who was a year senior to him.

I felt sorry for him. But I also knew that Jasraj was a very strong person. He would never let himself or anyone else feel sorry for him.

He was a great boss and a generous friend. It is not easy to have friends at work. You never know if the friendship is for work or the work is for friendship. In our case, we kept our boundaries clear. Work was work and friendship was friendship. There were many times I had to call Jasraj at odd hours for help. His contacts network was phenomenal and his willingness to help me without any hesitation was even more so.

I was happy to take up this new responsibility of managing the alliance with GLD as I knew it would make Jasraj happy. Not for the sake of work, but for the sake of our friendship.

For the next three and a half years or so, I did a great job of managing and implementing this alliance.

But working closely with GLD and understanding its finances better, I also knew that the company could get into trouble soon. I was happy that Aashu had resigned.

27

The first six months of the GLD alliance were spent in fine-tuning the details and translating the alliance into reality. What gets decided in the boardroom is not what necessarily gets implemented on the ground. My job was to ensure there was no gap between what was agreed between the promoters and what was finally achieved.

Anu was quite satisfied with our performance. She visited our sites in different cities and inspected the quality standards and progress of the project in great detail. She knew her business. Just as she knew what she wanted in her personal life.

During one of her visits to Bangalore, I happened to be in the city too. She came to know of this and invited me for dinner at her hotel.

I arrived at the hotel at the agreed time and called her room from the reception area.

"Hi Anu. I am here in the lobby."

"Hey Jeetu. I think it's better if we just order some room service in my suite. It will be much more convenient and give us the privacy to talk more openly about business."

I could hear the hum of a hummingbird in my head.

I knocked on the door of her suite. She opened it. She was wearing a short green mini skirt and a white shirt neatly tucked inside.

"Welcome to my humble suite."

I stepped inside the large suite, which looked more spacious thanks to the large glass windows on one side of the room. From the glass windows, I could see the green 18-hole golf course; a few people were playing in the night under lights.

Golf is a game of the mind, Jasraj often told me. He was passionate about golf. My meeting that day with Anu was a bigger game of the mind. And my sixth sense was on high alert.

"Come, let's sit down on the sofa, shall we?" She patted on the sofa where she was sitting.

I tried to sit far away from her. Her short skirt seemed even shorter when she was sitting. Her attractive legs seemed even longer.

"What do you want to drink?"

She reached for the mini bar on the side from where she was sitting and opened it. The bar was amply stocked with liquor and other additives. I chose my favourite combination of vodka and tonic water with Angostura bitters.

"Good choice, as always."

She got up and got the bottles out.

"Ah, I can make it myself..." I tried to intervene.

"You are my guest here. A special guest. And it's my special privilege to make your special drink."

I was not liking this 'special' night.

She poured a glass of red wine for herself and then sat down on the sofa again. This time much closer than before.

"So, are you satisfied with our performance, Anu?" I tried to steer her towards business.

"Depends on how you continue to *perform*...," she said seductively, with a wicked twist of the tongue when pronouncing the word 'perform'.

"Sure, I understand." I thought I understood her mood.

"Jeetu, I have a strong weakness. If I like something or like someone, then I make sure it becomes mine. I know you are married. But I have strong feelings for you."

Anu did not believe in wasting time in small talk. She came closer to me, her leg almost touching mine, and leaned forward towards my face.

I got up from the sofa.

"Anu, I am sorry. I can't do this. I have found my soulmate in my wife Aashu. And I will do nothing to even remotely jeopardise my relationship with her. You are a lovely and intelligent girl. You will get whoever you want, but as long as Aashu is alive in this lifetime or any other lifetime, I will be hers and hers only," I said, as calmly as I could.

Anu was an intelligent girl. And she had a smart eye for investments. She could also take quick calls. She realised that it would be a waste of her time to continue investing her feelings in me.

"Ouch! That hurts bad, Jeetu! But because I love you so much, I will let you be happy. I have never let anyone who has dared to hurt me live happily. But for you I will make an exception."

I was not sure if this was her heart or mind speaking. Anu knew that anyone else other than I could not manage the critical phase of alliance between Synfra and GLD.

She made sure that she did not let her feelings get in the way of business for the next three years. Synfra continued to work with GLD and I continued to do a good job. Meetings with Anu became far less frequent and only when necessary, and that too in the office environment.

I never told Aashu about this incident as I did not want to disturb her. And I was sure I had again passed the TFT test with flying colours.

28

Chachu was doing very well in his business as a transporter for the coal industry in Jharkhand. He had the right mix of business acumen, manpower support, and financial support from *baba*. I heard that he had a fleet of more than 1,000 trucks. I was happy for him and *choti chachi*. *Choti chachi* had always treated me well and whenever I was with her, I tried to not make her feel the loss of not having a child.

Our family suddenly became important among our relatives in the village. I was doing well in a corporate role and *chachu* was doing well in business. Relatives suddenly started remembering their 'closeness' and 'fondness' for us. I had a different theory of 'relative-ity' – the number of relatives you have is relative to your success. There is a constant factor, linked more to the blood line, and then there is a variable factor related directly to the volume of your success. Our variable factor was high at that time.

We were invited as special guests to most family functions. A second cousin of mine had a baby girl and he was very insistent that we attend her first birthday celebrations in Jamshedpur. My mother called me over phone.

"Son, you may not want to come, but sometimes as you grow up you have to do these things. The more the fruits on a tree, the more its branches bend down."

Winters were a pleasant time in Jamshedpur. There was a light cool breeze for most part of the day. Aashu had not been to Jamshedpur in a long time. *Baba, chachu* and *choti chachi* were also going to be there.

So we took the Rajdhani train, which stopped at Jamshedpur. We booked our tickets in the first class compartment as there were no other tickets available at short notice. We wanted to go by train and not take a flight. We perhaps wanted to recount the memories of the journey from where it all began.

After dinner on the train, we rolled out the bed sheets and pillow for Aarvee to sleep, on the upper berth. Aashu was to sleep with Aarvee and would go up later. There are just two berths in a compartment on the first class and there is a door to close the compartment for privacy.

After we made sure that Aarvee was deep in sleep, we pulled out a blanket that covered us both. We sat on the wide seat near the window. Aashu was resting her head on my shoulders and holding my hands.

"Jeetu, do you remember the first time we met? You seemed such an uptight person then."

"Really? I thought it was love at first sight for you!"

"Ha ha! It was anger at first sight!"

"Well if you were angry, then I must say you look prettier when angry. Or it has to be something about the trains that make you look prettier." I clenched her palm tight.

"What do you have in mind Mr Uptight who wanted love at first sight?" She was trying to rhyme words to make it more interesting.

Not to be outdone in rhyming, I shot back. "I want just love this night."

Poems have served as libido enhancers for both men and women for centuries. Our short attempt at poetry had the same effect on both of us. Aashu pushed me back a bit so that my head was lying on a pillow near the window while she rolled on top of me. She was wearing a *salwar kurta* while I was wearing a T-shirt and a track pant. I had already locked the door, in the faint hope of locking lips with Aashu later that night.

She was a woman on a mission. She gestured to me to be silent with a finger on her lips and whispered, "Sshh..."

She deftly removed her *salwar* and pushed it outside the blanket. Even more adroitly, she went inside the blanket briefly and emerged gleefully with my track pant in her hand, just like a scuba diver finding a hidden treasure from the depths of the ocean. We had already changed for the night and were wearing no undergarments. She was a woman on fire that day. Very different from the Aashu in bed usually. She glided herself into me and rode me in gentle rhythm, along with the motion of the train. We could hear the tea boy go and up down the alley in our coach; he even knocked on the door once. The fear and excitement of getting caught made our adrenaline flow stronger. We both climaxed together. I closed her mouth with my hands in anticipation of a loud outburst of passion at the end of the love ride.

Early next morning, the train slowly drew into the Tatanagar railway station where my parents were waiting for us.

We both touched my parents' feet as soon as we got down the railway platform. My father asked Aashu, "Hope the journey was pleasurable, Aashu?"

"Oh yes, *papa*. It was very pleasurable."

We both looked at each other and winked.

On the first night of our stay at Jamshedpur, I again had a dream which I remembered the next morning. I told Aashu about it.

"What are you saying, Jeetu? I pray to God this one remains just a dream."

"I even remember the hotel name in Bistupur. It was called Boulevard, where I saw *chachu* having an extramarital affair with some young woman."

Bistupur was the main market area in Jamshedpur and Hotel Boulevard was at the start of the main road in the market. Boulevard had a well-known restaurant and some rooms for staying too.

Whenever I visited Jamshedpur, I called my old friends from school and we would meet somewhere for a drink. I envied the easy life of my friends. They would come back from work by 6 p.m. and then meet at one of the many upscale clubs in Jamshedpur, have a drink or two, sometimes dinner with their wives, go back home, and be in bed by 9.30 p.m.

This time, we wanted to do something more adventurous than going to the clubs. So, we chose to go to Hotel Boulevard.

Chachu, choti chachi, and *baba* had arrived a couple of days earlier than we had and were staying at my parents' house. *Baba* and *choti* chachi had decided to visit a famous temple near Ranchi the day we arrived and spend a couple of days at *choti chachi's* sister's place in Ranchi. As *chachu* had some business in Jamshedpur, he decided to stay back. My *choti chachi's* sister had insisted that *baba* also come and stay with them in Ranchi.

Four friends met in the evening at Boulevard. Aashu was not too fond of these meetings as she knew it was meant for boys only. And when the boys meet, the talk is focussed on girls. Girls of the past usually.

We entered the hotel. I saw a couple climb up the stairs to the first floor where the rooms were located. I turned and looked again. It was *chachu* with a young wheatish complexioned woman. *Chachu* was holding her tight while she giggled.

The rest of the evening was a blur to me. I smiled when the others did and laughed when I saw my friends laughing. I was dying to go back home and speak to the only person who would not consider me insane.

Aashu was dumbfounded when I narrated the incident to her.

"What are you going to do now, Jeetu?"

"Let me think. I will do what's right for the family."

I went to bed early that night.

Next morning, *choti chachi* and *baba* arrived together with Bhola. I was so happy to see them. It had been a very long trip. *Baba* was looking healthier than before. He had fought cancer bravely like his many other enemies and he had won again.

"Jeetu, my star! I feel 10 years younger every time I see you. So, if you want your *baba* to live long, come and see me more often." I went and put my head on his laps as he lovingly caressed my hair.

Choti chachi was looking as young and as fresh as I had last seen her, many years ago. How could *chachu* do this to her? She was so much more beautiful than that other woman. And so devoted and committed. *Baba* was fully dependent on her now for daily chores. Men can indeed be dogs – ungrateful dogs.

I did what was right for the family. A family should uphold its values and culture and protect its children and women. *Choti chachi* was as much family to me as *chachu* was. I told her everything.

"Aashu, I did what was right for the family. For *choti chachi's* nest. Our nest. I told her everything."

"What? How did she react?" Aashu was genuinely shocked.

"She was shocked too. And sad. She didn't want to believe it at first. But since I had seen him with my own eyes, she knew she could trust me fully. She is leaving for her sister's place in Ranchi later this evening. She will never disclose how she came to know this. Bhola is going to go with her."

It was good to see Bhola. Bhola looked as strong as ever, though he had more grey hairs this time.

"How are you, Bhola?" I asked him while he waited outside our house for *choti chachi* to come out and take the autorickshaw to the bus stand.

"Going on as usual, Jeetu sir. So good to see you always. Sir, I wanted one help from you. If you don't mind. There is a young boy, having a licence for a pistol also. Well-built. But only 10th pass. If you can get him to join your security company in some good position, I will be very grateful." Bhola requested with folded hands.

"Oh, that's nothing, Bhola. Please take this card and tell him to call my office. And my assistant will take care of the rest."

With all this happening, my second cousin's event was a low-key affair for our family. We met many other relatives at the celebrations. I enquired about Neha *didi*. It was then my mother told me what had happened to her over the past few years.

"It's very sad, Jeetu. Neha's husband became an alcoholic. He drank and beat her every day. In front of their son. This went on for months, years. Finally, she could take it no more and one night she left her house with her son. And she took the train to Patna where her brother is a principal in a school. I believe Neha is now a teacher in the same school. She lives with her brother. She has not even filed for divorce. She just wanted to get away from her husband, that brute."

I could see tears roll down my mother's cheeks as she talked.

Choti chachi was no such pushover. She may not have been educated from a premier college or even been to a large city. But she had the heart of a true Indian woman. The heart to give everything for someone she loved and the heart to take away everything from someone she loathed.

When we came back to Delhi, my father informed me that *choti chachi* had moved back to her house in our village. After discussing with *baba,* she had filed for a divorce. *Baba* had confronted *chachu* soon after he was made aware of *chachu's* infidelity. He was convinced that *choti chachi* was right. From then on, he fully supported *choti chachi* through everything. He asked *chachu* to leave the house.

Choti chachi now lives in our ancestral house with *baba* and takes care of him like before.

29

GLD was in a big financial trouble. It had taken loans at very high interest rates from some large domestic investors and was unable to pay them back due to poor sales. The investors were naturally very angry and started exploring every possible way to get their money back. Karan Grover had mortgaged most of his shares in GLD to these investors. But since GLD was not a listed company, these shares were just plain papers until somebody paid for them. The investors were looking out for a white knight.

Synfra had gained a lot of knowledge about GLD's projects and had the ability to accurately forecast the costs and revenues for GLD. This was an advantage that Jasraj leveraged when the GLD investors came to him to buy the GLD shares.

"Gentlemen, these papers are useless if GLD and the market do not turn around. How can I pay you anything for them? I would need some working capital from you, so that I can run the GLD business efficiently and then maybe pay you back." Jasraj was as shrewd a negotiator as one could find.

"Mr Jasraj, we are in no mood or position to put more money into GLD. But we can consider selling our shares for a discount to our principal loan value, leave aside the interest part." The investors discussed openly with Jasraj.

This was the opening Jasraj was looking for. He swooped down on the gullible investors like a vulture and took a large pound of flesh from them. The investors finally settled for selling at 50 per cent of the principal loan value. Something was better for them than nothing. Jasraj gained control of GLD at a fraction of its intrinsic enterprise value.

Anu was mad when she came to know of this and immediately called a battery of lawyers to challenge this transaction. She wanted to sue Jasraj. Given a choice, she would have preferred to kill him. But she was rightly advised that she would end up fighting a long losing battle. She called for a press conference where her disdain for Jasraj was amply demonstrated.

"Jasraj is a vulture of the worst kind. He is the kind of vulture you try and help when it is injured. You grow close to it and allow it to live in your house. And then, one night when you are sleeping, the vulture comes and plucks your eyes out. That's Mr Jasraj for you, folks."

She was correct in a way. But business is a game played by vultures, not cute-looking rabbits.

Just after the press conference, I received a call from Anu.

"Jeetu, you have backstabbed me. I did not expect more than friendship from you. But you decided to not even honour the friendship part." She was clearly very hurt.

"Anu, I am sorry. But I was not aware of Jasraj's plans. He did ask me about GLD's projects and the numbers involved, but I never knew it would come to this." I tried to defend myself.

"You can continue to take sides with Jasraj. But remember, a day will come when he will cut you slowly with a knife made of sugar and you will not even realise it. Anyway, that's your call. My call is not to see you in my life again. Goodbye and have a happy life." She disconnected the phone without letting me speak.

Anu had already floated a separate subsidiary for the hospitality business and had made alliances with some large international hotel chains. She was going to focus on that business. I was sure she would do well.

Synfra was a company having interests in development, construction and operations all under one roof. No other real estate or infrastructure company in India had such a breadth of skills and integrated businesses. Luckily for Jasraj, the real estate market started picking up rapidly after this deal, and Synfra continued its growth with even more rapid strides.

For the next five years, I worked like a dog for Synfra and Jasraj. I was rewarded well too. I got a million-dollar bonus in the next two years. We bought a larger apartment in Gurgaon and moved there. Unfortunately, along with the size of our apartment, the size of my waist was also increasing. I was angry with myself for having ignored my health for so long. This was the only negative aspect I could think of in my relationship with Aashu. We were both so madly in love with each other and committed to each other that we forgot to take care of ourselves. There was no threat of our mutual attraction diminishing in any way. And without a threat, human beings tend to become lazy and careless.

But there was a larger threat looming. We were not as active as before. We did not party as much as before. We did not go out and play games with Aarvee. Sex became more of a routine chore. This had to change.

I joined the gym in our apartment complex and also bought high-end equipment for exercising at home. Within a year, we lost about 10 per cent of the additional weight we had gained and felt younger again. Investing in one's health is without doubt the most important and lucrative investment one can make in life.

"Let's go somewhere for a week to celebrate this, Jeetu?"

"And gain all that weight back again?"

"No, let's go to a place where there is healthy food, healthy air, and healthy activities to do."

A friend of mine had just returned from a privately managed organic farm of 200 acres in Dehradun. And he was all praise for it. It was quite expensive though. It would cost us a few lakh rupees for a week.

"That costly? Let's leave it then. Better to buy Aarvee an X-Box and diamond solitaires for me with that money. These things will last far more than a week and keep us happy for a longer time." Aashu tried to convince me.

"What is wrong with you? Life is all about the experiences you have. These experiences make you wiser and bring you closer to family. These experiences give you a lifetime of memories and happiness. How can you compare it with material gadgets? The value of such experiences can only appreciate, whereas these gadgets only have depreciating value." I had some strong opinions on this matter.

We finally did go to the Dehradun farm. It was a beautiful open space with lots of mango trees. Organic farming was practised here. It also had a dairy farm. We did a lot of cycling together in the dirt tracks within the farm. Aarvee also enjoyed himself and he went cycling with us.

On the second day of our visit, Aarvee's cycle skid and he fell down on the bushes on the side of the tracks. He had some bruises on his leg. Aashu and I were so worried that we took a cab and went to the nearby hospital. The doctor laughed at us when he saw the bruise and advised us to just wash it and put a band-aid on it.

One worries so much for children than for his or her parents. Both children and parents are close to us but the protective feeling is much more for children. I don't think it is only because children are dependent upon us fully, it is also because we know our children will be the carriers of our genes in the future. And we want to live forever through these genes. I wished Aashu and I were a pair of inseparable genes that got passed on and on and lived together forever and ever.

"I am so glad you made us come here," Aashu thanked me towards the end of the trip. She continued. "You know, I always used to think that the passion, romance and fire in our relationship would gradually fade with the passage of time after marriage. But I now believe that real romance sets in only after living together for many years – when you know every layer of the other person, when you know what he or she means or does not mean, when you know exactly what a particular facial expression is, and when you know that whatever happens you will always be the parents of your child."

She became emotional saying this.

"Aashu, for me love is like old wine. Gets better with age. Love is like Tendulkar. Gives more pleasure as it grows older."

She grinned and showed her pearly white teeth. Her brown eyes sparkled at the same time. She could still mesmerise me in an instant.

We had to return to Delhi by the next morning as there was a large celebratory party being thrown by Jasraj. Aashu never liked attending these office parties. "What will I do talking to Jasraj? Let him get married and then I will come to these parties and talk to his wife."

30

Baba was not keeping well after *chachu* and *chachi* separated. My father had taken him to the hospital in Bombay again and the doctors said that the cancer had suddenly spread and was in an advanced stage. He could survive for a year at least but not more than two years.

Cancer's main nutrients are worry, anxiety, sadness and grief. It loves to feed on these attributes and grows rapidly. The genes want to live but when the inner fire charging these genes starts to fade, then the cancer raises its fangs with full fury. *Baba's* inner fire was fading. He was no longer the *baba* we all feared and respected at the same time. He kept to himself mostly. He sometimes spoke to Bhola in grief.

I was very disturbed with this news. I often woke up in the middle of the night, sweating profusely and gasping for breath. But I did not remember anything of what I had dreamt.

Then one night, when I woke up, I remembered the dream. An old lady had come in my dream. She asked me to sit up. She then took a pen and wrote on a piece of paper: *Baba* 922, in Hindi. She told me that this would be the date when *baba* would leave his mortal body.

I told Aashu and my mother about the dream the next day. They both asked me to think positively and forget about the dream, although Aashu and my mother were aware that many of my dreams in the recent past had turned out to be true.

We forgot about this dream. *Baba* was again recovering well, but suddenly his health deteriorated and he passed away, almost like the last flicker of a candle flame. I received the call from my mother early in the morning. It was February 12. I cried like a baby and kept howling "*baba, baba*." Aashu consoled me and held me in her arms like a baby. She said, "*Baba* would not like to see you cry. Be strong. And make his name stronger."

I took the next available flight to Ranchi that day. On the flight, the person sitting on my right was reading a Hindi newspaper. He was reading the middle pages. The front page of the paper was pointed towards me. I looked at it and my eyes wandered around the Hindi words and then settled on the top of the page in which the date of the paper was printed in Hindi - 92/2. Number 9 in the English system looks very similar to numeric 1 in Hindi; number 2 in the English system and Hindi are written more or less in the same style.

I was shocked beyond belief. My mind immediately remembered the date written by the old lady in my dream a couple of months ago. It was the same date that *baba* died. I spent the rest of the flight with my hands folded and my eyes glued to the blue sky, waiting for some divine intervention to make me more learned.

Science had taught me to believe in a hypothesis after several observations over a sustained number of data points. My dreams over the last several years had established my hypothesis that there was a clear link between my dreams and reality. But the science I had learnt had no explanation for this. I could only speculate. Probably the neurons in my brain were able to penetrate the other dimensions of the universe during the dream, in which time was running faster than the time in our three-dimensional world.

I had by now turned into a confused believer from a non-believer. It would take a fair time before I turned into a full believer.

For now, Jasraj was a full believer in me. He continued to give me more responsibilities and perks and I helped grow the business in the next 2-3 years. Aashu took great care of Aarvee as a mother during my absence from home. Aarvee was growing up to be a good and talented boy who had no rebellious streaks of his father.

Aashu was showing signs of boredom. She was also a bit frustrated. I suggested she take up some hobby. She decided to learn painting and went for a month-long class in painting.

"So, how's your painting class going?" I asked her over dinner.

"It's already over, dear. I have to start practising on my own now."

"And have you started that?' I enquired.

"Have some more noodles. I have put a lot of vegetables in it."

She had prepared chilly chicken and noodles, one of my favourite dishes. She was also not prepared to answer my question directly.

"Aashu, have you started painting on your own?" I persisted.

She looked a bit embarrassed and then replied. "Yes. I started with a lot of zeal and also created a folder on your desktop computer with a password to scan and store all my paintings. I started to think of myself as the next Hussain and believed my drawings would make millions." Even in embarrassment, Aashu never lost her sense of humour.

"But after I drew and saved my first painting, I realised that it is not something that I enjoy at all."

"Then don't do it. Period!" I said emphatically. "Is there anything else you are interested in?" I asked.

"Jeetu, I have been thinking for a while now. You have all this experience in construction and services and development also now. I have some good experience in finance and marketing. Why don't we do something in real estate of our own?"

Her eyes suddenly lit up.

"Like what, Aashu?"

"Think of your 5 Ps theory. You now have 3 Ps already. *Paisa* (money), *power*, *pyaar* (love). Your life is anyways full of your 4th P - pictures; we have enjoyed so many movies already. That leaves you with the 5th P – *pahad* (mountains). We should do something for your 5th P. Let's do an exclusive holiday home real estate project somewhere in the hills."

I had just been handed a bonus of 100 million rupees by Jasraj and I was doing very well financially. We had a good house and all the other comforts of life. Maybe it was time to move out of my comfort zone and explore the boundaries.

"Yes, let's do it!" I almost shouted in excitement.

Aashu hugged me tight. I knew she wanted to say 'thank you' but could not.

31

The next morning, we had our morning tea in the balcony of our apartment. Aashu stood up from her chair and as she turned to open the door of the balcony leading to the house, I could not but steal a quick glance at the shapely mound of flesh below her waist tightly wrapped in a green cotton sari. She was nearing 40 but could still stir wild emotions in me.

We had a sumptuous lunch of chicken curry and brown rice and then decided to take some rest in the afternoon. We had a long night ahead of us. We had to go to Jasraj's reception party after his wedding to a social entrepreneur, Rakhi, a few days ago.

Jasraj was in his late thirties now. He had realised that he would soon need a progeny to carry on the vast empire he had built over the last decade. Jasraj was already very well known in the business circles and was also very active in politics and philanthropy. I had teased him once, "Jasraj, India needs you. You don't need a family – you should adopt the whole of India as your family!"

"I can help in the planning of this country but not in the planning of its family," he retorted in his usual witty style.

"I just hate the way the population of this country keeps growing. The country gets more mouths to feed and politicians get more mouths they need. More mouths to shout their caste-based slogans. More mouths of sycophants who sing their false praises." Jasraj had a clear disdain for politicians.

"Well, this country needs politicians like you, Jasraj," I said.

"This country needs a benevolent dictator to start with. Someone who transforms himself or herself into a socialist worker." Jasraj may have been a capitalist by birth but he was a socialist at heart.

Hence, it was no surprise to me when I first heard about Rakhi from Jasraj.

"I went out for lunch with an amazing woman today. She is an MBA from Cornell and belongs to a rich landlord family from Punjab. She had a very high paying corporate job with a multinational bank. And then she threw it all and decided to join an NGO. An NGO that helps trace missing children. And let me tell you, she is beautiful!"

"That is indeed a very noble thing she is doing. I will now know where to go to when Aarvee goes missing." I always knew how to spoil the mood.

"Jeetu, do you know how many children go missing in our country every day? And do you know how many of them are traced? The police have so many things to manage in this country that they cannot find the time to find the most important thing for any citizen – his or her child!" Jeetu was clearly flustered by my earlier response.

"So, while most of us just sit in front of the TV and talk about it or have a glass of wine in our hands and exchange views on it in a social party, Rakhi actually took up the cause of her maid's missing girl with the local police. It was then she realised the magnitude of this malaise and decided to join this NGO."

Jeetu was as much excited about meeting Rakhi as he was by her cause.

I did not think it was prudent to remind Jeetu about his school crush. He seemed happy and he definitely needed a partner in his journey. Rakhi was an apt choice for Jasraj. Jasraj had always made the right choices.

Rakhi had shared a very interesting story to Jasraj recently about which Jasraj told me last week.

"Do you know about Anu?" Jasraj asked me.

"Not really. Last I heard she was doing well in her hospitality business."

"Oh, then you should really hear this. Anu married a rich politician in Delhi about a year ago. And then the politician cheated on her. Do you know with whom? Their maid! The maid got pregnant with the politician's child. And when Anu found out about this, she divorced him. And she made him marry the maid." Jeetu was in splits narrating this.

"And then our Anu ensured that this politician did not get a ticket to stand in the coming elections. So, right now this one-time rich, famous, and powerful politician is married to his maid, holding a baby in his hand that he does not want, with no power or position in society. This is what Anu Grover can do to you, Jeetu. Beware of her wrath!"

I had no reason to fear Anu's wrath. Her enemy was Jasraj, not me. But during the drive to the reception party later that night, I could not help wonder about the irony between Jasraj meeting Rakhi due to a maid and Anu getting divorced, again due to a maid. Relationships are indeed made or broken in strange circumstances.

The party was in Jasraj's sprawling farmhouse in Vasant Kunj area. We reached well on time as usual, when there were hardly any guests at the venue. In Delhi, it's impolite to reach the host's place on time because the host is not expecting you on time. Those who reached on time were considered to have no other work or engagements. But Jasraj was aware of my habits. He knew I preferred to come in early, have dinner early, and leave early so that I could go to sleep early, and then finally rise early.

The arrangements at the farmhouse were elaborate. The entire garden was adorned with bright fresh flowers. Seating arrangements were made under several temporary gazebos wrapped in smooth, silky pink and white coloured sheets. The gazebos were lit with candles inside lamps hanging from the four corners of the structure.

"This is very impressive!" Aashu was not someone to be easily impressed.

"Yes, Jasraj does have style. And, of course, the money to afford the style!" I remarked.

After about half an hour, we saw the lovely looking couple, walking, hand in hand, into the main garden area where more guests had assembled by then. Jasraj was looking dashing as ever and Rakhi was matching him well in style, grace, and looks. They did make a great couple.

We walked up to them.

"Hi Jasraj. Hi Rakhi. My formal congratulations to both of you." I shook hands with Jasraj warmly and folded my hands to greet Rakhi.

"And this is my wife, Aashu." I introduced Aashu to both Jasraj and Rakhi for the first time.

"*Namaste*. My heartiest congratulations! You both look a match made in heaven." Aashu smiled and wished them.

Rakhi thanked us both for coming and insisted we meet again soon at their house. Jasraj was surprisingly a bit silent. Perhaps he realised that he was actually in a legal commitment. And that can be a scary thought for many men. Especially men who had gotten used to living a single life for a long time.

"Good to meet you, Aashu *ji*. Jeetu has taken a long time in introducing us. We should have met much before," said Jasraj, looking at Aashu. Jasraj hardly addressed anybody with the respectful '*ji*' and I was pleasantly surprised.

We had an early dinner and then left. On the drive back, we crossed the place where we lived when we had just come to Delhi. We both looked at each other knowingly and held hands with a light squeeze. We may not have the money, the style, or a sprawling farmhouse like Jasraj and Rakhi, but we sure did have a lot of love between us, even after so many years of marriage.

32

A month passed after Jasraj's wedding reception. It was a Sunday morning, and we did not get up early. We decided to just laze in bed a bit longer. Aashu snuggled up to me and rested her head on my arms and her legs on my stomach. She was smelling like she did when I first saw her on the train and at the Durga *puja pandal*.

"How can you smell so lovely early in the morning?" I complained.

"You know when I am happy, I look and smell better. Maybe my happy glands are linked to my sweat glands."

"And why are you so happy today?" I enquired.

"Because in two days, we will be starting the journey of the next phase of our life together." Aashu was referring to our planned visit to Uttaranchal for identifying a suitable piece of land for our project.

"I love you," she whispered into my ears.

It still was a thrill to hear those words from her. I knew her love was unconditional and not because I had decided to do this project together with her. She loved me because she just loved me. Simple.

My thoughts drifted to Anu Grover then. I felt a bit sorry for her. She definitely deserved better. Did Anu really love me? How was her love for me different from Aashu's? I cursed myself for even making this comparison in my mind. Why do human beings enjoy the thought of several people from the opposite sex loving them? Is it because it makes us feel more desirable or is it because it provides more options to us in life to spread our genes? I quickly banished these thoughts from my mind. Aashu loved me because of who I was. Anu loved me because of who she was. If I had reciprocated her feelings, then Anu would have loved herself more. Because she had managed to make me love her.

Trying to link the thoughts of the brain to the feelings of the heart can be a very complicated and confusing exercise. I left it at that.

"Where are you lost again, Jeetu?" Aashu hated it when I went into my silent thinking zone.

"Oh, nothing. Nothing worthwhile at least. Let us start planning soon for our visit to Gazaar," I replied and kissed her softly on the forehead.

A former colleague of Aashu from her GLD days had informed Aashu about this 50 acres of land in Gazaar, a small village about 60 km uphill from Bhimtaal. The landowner was a local villager who had done well in life and subsequently moved to Dubai to run a logistics company. He had no family left in India and was not keen on keeping this land.

Aashu's colleague had introduced us over email to Atul Katiyal, a broker from a small city called Haldwani near the base of the lower Himalayan hills, about a four-hour drive from Gazaar. Atul was representing the landowner in the potential sale of the land in Gazaar.

I had discussed with Jasraj the previous week about my plans for the project. At first, he did not seem happy about it. But then he thought a bit, and said, "Jeetu, you are not just my manager but also my friend. I will do whatever is good for you and Aashu *ji*. If you want, I can even help in some funding for this project. But it would be good if you can continue as a part-time advisor at least with Synfra for the next couple of years." I could not say no to Jasraj.

My parents were with us in Delhi at that time. So we were not worried about Aarvee. We had planned on leaving very early in the morning and having lunch with Atul Katiyal at a resort near Gazaar. We would then visit the site in the late afternoon and stay for the night in the resort. Early next morning, we were to drive back to Delhi.

It was going to be a tiring couple of days but we were excited as this was our first entrepreneurial effort. There is always a different thrill and excitement when one works for oneself. You get the feeling of being a master of your own destiny. But the true master of everyone's destiny often has different plans.

It was a very long drive to Gazaar via Moradabad and Rampur and then through Haldwani, Kathgodam, Bhimtaal. Fortunately, we had a comfortable SUV and our driver was very experienced and reliable. A lot of construction work was going on for flyovers and bridges and wide-laning the stretch from Delhi to Kathgodam. Kathgodam was the base from where we started climbing the hills. Aashu was at ease and relaxed during the whole journey.

"Why do you look so hassled?" She asked.

"These roads seem to be always getting built and rebuilt. It's good for the future, I am sure. But what about the present?" I was visibly upset.

"You are being selfish and thinking about yourself only."

"No, I am not. It's just that the present of the future will also have the same issues."

"What? I don't get it?"

"I mean that in future too, it will continue like this. People will have the same issues in future too. It's a never-ending cycle. And you know why? Because our population keeps increasing so rapidly. So, we have to keep building these roads. I completely agree with Jasraj that the growing population is a bane for this country."

Aashu laughed out aloud.

"Jeetu, I can see that Jasraj has really influenced you. What you and Jasraj are conveniently forgetting is that a lot of Synfra's growth has happened due to this growing population. The roads you are complaining about today are the roads you were building till very recently." Aashu always had a valid point. I did not complain much for the rest of the journey.

As we crossed Bhimtaal Lake, I could see it was half-dry but it still looked majestic with the shadows of the trees lining the lake and the sun's rays shimmering on the surface.

"Do you know how this lake was formed?" Aashu asked me.

"Yes, I think I know. It's probably due to some chain of faults in the earth's crust?" I was still an engineer in mind first.

"No. The local people say that when the Pandavas were in exile, Draupadi was very thirsty one day. She asked the strong Pandava, Bhim, to fetch water for her. Bhim came to this place and hit the ground so hard with his mace that the water gushed out and went on to form this lake," Aashu said, with a pretty straight face.

"And when I feel thirsty at home, you won't not even get up and get me a glass of water!" She poked me in jest.

"Goddesses like you are meant to have only nectar, not earthly water from my hands." I hoped to get away with this.

"Jeetu, when I die, at least then put a drop of water on my parched lips. I will make the rest of the journey upwards thinking it was nectar from you."

I put my fingers on her lips asking her to speak no more. I could not bear the thought of Aashu being away from me even for a day. And she was talking of eternal separation! Even when I travelled, I made sure I called or 'skyped' her every four hours. I was sure there was some internal body formula – four hours was the maximum time my mind and heart could tolerate her absence for. If I was travelling within India, I made sure to come back after one night and then again travel the next day if needed. As much as possible, I avoided international travel precisely for this reason.

"Will you marry someone else if I die?" Aashu asked. She was in no mood to steer away from this topic.

"No," I replied curtly.

"What will you do then?" she asked.

"Wait for the next lifetime to meet you again."

She became silent after that and was lost in her thoughts, the hills, and the romantic songs playing in the car.

33

"Sir. Ma'am. So glad to meet you finally in person... in person. I am Atul Katiyal… Atul Katiyal." Atul greeted us at the main entrance of the lobby of the resort. He had recognised us from the car number we had given to him in advance.

Atul was short and quite overweight, with a protruding beer belly and a few strands of curly grey hair. He must have been in his mid-thirties. What was most striking about his appearance was the extraordinarily dark complexion, made darker by the several grotesque pimples on his face. He was not an attractive man at first sight.

"How was your journey… your journey?" he asked us politely. We both quickly realised that Atul had this weird habit of repeating the last couple of words of his sentences.

Atul read what was going on in our minds.

"I know what you must be thinking… must be thinking. Why do I repeat my words… my words? I am sorry but it's a hereditary problem… hereditary problem. Some doctors call it palilalia condition… palilalia condition," Atul explained to us.

"Oh, that's not a problem at all. None of us are born perfect." Aashu tried to make him comfortable. I knew Aashu was lying though. She was born perfect.

We went inside the restaurant for lunch. There was no one in there other than us. I guessed that the people in the hills didn't come to such restaurants for meals. And those who came to the resort must have been busy with outdoor activities at that time of the day.

"Ma'am. I have already ordered some rice and chicken curry, some noodles and chilly chicken… chilly chicken."

We were ecstatic to have our favourite meals served in this far-flung place. The food was excellent, with local flavours.

"Ma'am. You must be cooking much better than this… than this." Atul sure knew how to please Aashu.

After lunch, we climbed into our SUV. Atul sat in the front seat. He gave directions to our driver to the site we had come to visit. The roads in the hills were much better than those we had seen in the plains. I took pride in explaining to Aashu that this was because the water never gets collected on the roads in the hills. It's like the perfect natural draining system.

We drove for about half an hour when we saw a cemented road on the right. Atul pointed to our driver to take that road. The cemented road was narrow with dense trees on both sides. It was very steep. We soon came out to an open area on top of a hillock. It was surrounded by forests on all sides.

"This is the site… the site. Look at the forests and snow-covered hills all around… all around."

From where we stood, we could have a 270-degree view of the snow-clad mountain ranges.

"That one is Nanda Devi... Nanda Devi. And one on this side is Trishul... is Trishul." Atul pointed in the direction of the mountains.

The forests around us were filled with pine, deodar, and silver oak trees and looked like a wave of green shades rising up and down.

"Ma'am. Before the summers, you get these beautiful red flowers on these rhododendron trees... rhododendron trees. You can eat them too... eat them too. Or you can put them in your beautiful black hair... black hair."

"Ha ha. Well put, Atul. By the way, are there animals in these forests too?" Aashu asked Atul.

"There are lots of animals in these forests like deer, bears and leopards... and leopards. But nothing to worry about... worry about. They stay deep in the forests below and hardly come up to this level... this level."

We were falling in love with the place. It was what we had dreamt of. Lush green meadows, forests all around, and snow-covered mountains watching us.

The sun was about to set and we could see the changing colours on the mountains. There was a golden colour shine on the snow-white peaks giving the impression of a large inverted vanilla ice-cream cone with caramel topping. We had not seen or experienced anything like that ever before.

"Atul, can we come back here tomorrow morning again to take a proper look?" I asked. We wanted to understand the site better and plan accordingly.

"Sure sir… sure sir!"

I was not sure whether this time it was his speech condition or mere excitement.

We went back to the resort just as the stars were coming out. Atul was staying in some cheaper hotel nearby and bid us goodbye with the promise to see us just after breakfast the next day. The resort had a large garden on the terrace, which overlooked a deep valley. There were a couple of wrought iron benches in the garden, with a cute looking lamp post near them. After dinner, we decided to go up to the terrace. It was very cold but we had anticipated that and brought warm clothes with us. As we went out in the open garden area, we could see the sky above brightly lit by billions of glimmering stars.

It was indeed a spectacle to marvel about. We occasionally saw a shooting star running across the canvas of the sky. We also confused a plane flying at a high altitude or a satellite to a slow moving star. Amid the billions of stars, the moon held its place high and mighty. It was a full moon day and I could almost reach out and catch the moon. It seemed so large and near. I could also see the craters on the moon with my bare naked eyes.

We sat on the bench. I wrapped my arms around Aashu's shoulders and pulled her closely towards me. The diffused yellow light from the lamp post, the bright white light of the stars above, and the distant flickering lights from the small huts in the valley below together created a truly magical sensation.

"I think there is no other place called heaven. Earth is actually heaven. We just don't realise it," Aashu said, with a slightly mysterious sigh.

"You are right. But the Earth is both heaven and hell. Depends on what state of mind you are in. And I am glad if it is indeed this way. I would rather meet you again in the next lifetime on this planet than anywhere else," I said.

"Why, what's wrong in meeting in some other planet?" Aashu turned towards me and her eyebrows narrowed.

"Well, I don't want to take any chances! I don't know what might be in store in some other planet. Maybe there are giant talking lizards there who make human beings their slaves or maybe you have to live under water all your life with the fishes as your friends. I am not taking any chance with you, my dear."

"Brilliant, my IIT engineer! You have first of all assumed the probability of meeting in another lifetime as humans. What theory of yours is that? Yes, yes, I remember, the Point Ten Zeros Six Nine theory! But now you are saying you don't want to take any chance. What logic is this?" Aashu was at her logical best.

"Good point, my smart angel! See, we would have already tested the extremities of the probability theory by meeting in the next lifetime as humans. Why take further chances?"

"Good answer. I like it." Aashu patted me on the back.

34

Early next morning, we had breakfast in the balcony of our rooms, watching the sun shine on the snow peaks. The morning sun exposed the cracks and crevices and the mud colour on the snow much more than the evening sun. But the mountains still looked beautiful. As beautiful as Aashu when she woke up in the morning with no make-up on her face.

Atul was on time as promised, wearing a bright T-shirt and black jeans. I was beginning to like Atul. In fact, I was a little sympathetic towards him for his lack of physical attractiveness and his speech condition. He seemed an honest, sincere, hard-working, and helpful person.

On the drive to the site, I tried to find more about Atul.

"So Atul, tell us more about yourself. How did you get into this deal and what do you do in general?"

"Oh sir, it's a long story... long story. I will try and say it in short though... short though. I was born and brought up in Delhi where my father was a government official... government official. I did my schooling and graduation there and also did an MBA from FMS Delhi… FMS Delhi."

"Oh, you are an MBA too? That's great, and that too from a prestigious college like FMS." I was a bit surprised.

"Yes sir, I might not look like an MBA … an MBA. But I worked for many years in a reputed leasing company before I ventured out on my own… my own. I invested in a few projects and businesses but all of them failed because the promoters were big cheats… big cheats. I lost a lot of money during that period… that period. And after that, I decided to earn some quick money and got in touch with a few landowners to sell their lands… their lands."

"Very sorry to hear that. I can realise how painful that must have been. But hope you have not lost faith in humanity and people. Trust me, there are more good people than there are bad people on this earth. Otherwise, the earth would come to a halt with the bad people overpowering the good people and then fighting among themselves. Forget it, me and my logic! Tell me, where do you live now and what about your family?"

"Sir, I live in Haldwani now and I sometimes go to Delhi… to Delhi. I am a widower and I lost my wife to blood cancer five years ago… five years ago. Fortunately, we had no children… no children."

"That is so sad, Atul. I am really very sorry for you. You are a brave man who continues to fight after all these major setbacks in life," said Aashu. Her eyes were watery as she said this.

"Thank you ma'am... thank you ma'am. I had once thought of committing suicide also... suicide also. But a priest told me that God gives more trouble in the next lifetime to those who commit suicide... commit suicide. I wanted to make sure all my troubles and miseries end with this lifetime itself...lifetime itself," Atul said with a very serious face.

Aashu and I looked at each other from the corner of our eyes. We were glad to be doing business with someone like Atul who had values similar to ours, was god-fearing, and also believed in the next lifetime.

On the way, there was a small temple built on the rocks of the mountain slopes. Atul requested the driver to stop. He got out and knelt down in front of the temple chanting some prayers.

When he returned, Aashu asked him, "What were you chanting Atul and what does that mean?"

"Ma'am, my grandfather who used to live with us in Delhi was a very saintly person... saintly person. He used to pray for more than eight hours every day... every day. He taught me these special chants... special chants. It's difficult to explain it but it basically means make your life useful to others... to others. And help others who are in need... in need. And in doing so, may one achieve true salvation... true salvation."

God had a strange way of punishing good people with misery and pain, and rewarding bad people with fame and money. We felt sorry for Atul and his pain but we were glad that he had not lost his faith yet in people or god.

We reached the site and took a walk around the entire perimeter of the area. As we walked around it, we mentally sketched the project and the location of the villas, the landscaping, and the common entertainment area. We were happy to find out that there was ample underground water; there was also electricity in the neighbouring parcels of the village.

What about the dense forests all around the site and partly within the site, we wondered.

"Atul, will this site be allowed for an eco-friendly development project as the forests are so near?" Aashu asked Atul.

"Not an issue at all… at all. I had thought of this… of this. I had gone to the hill development authorities and they gave me a letter that this area will not come under the notified forest area; we are allowed to do low-rise villas here… villas here. Just no cutting of trees please… trees please."

Atul showed us the letter from the authorities. I read it in detail and I was satisfied.

Aashu and I decided to take a walk in the forests nearby. We requested Atul to wait at the site itself. There was a narrow path in the forests made by the local villagers. We continued to walk on that path, and the trees got denser and denser. The sound of the forest, the chirping of the birds, and the occasional glimpse of the sun through the gaps in the trees made the setting very romantic. And it brought back memories. I stopped Aashu on the path and kissed her passionately. She was not the least taken by surprise and happily contributed to the locking of the lips.

"I had to do this, Aashu. Brought back memories of our first kiss," I reminded her.

"My love. The moment we walked into the forest, I knew what was coming. I am glad you have not changed after all these years." And she laughed aloud.

"Yes, forests are the safest places to kiss and make love. You know why? Because our immunity goes up multifold because of the mist emitted from these trees, which contain special oils." I sounded like an expert on trees and forests.

"Jeetu, it's safe for us to kiss anywhere. You don't need to come to the forests for that. But I liked the feel of all that mist and oils on your lips." And she laughed again.

We started walking back towards the site; Aashu stopped to pick up some pine cones on the path. As she got up, we heard a sudden rustling in the bushes and a deer crossed our path on to the other side. It was our first real experience of the wild and we both shouted with joy. My joy quickly turned into fear when I remembered Atul talking about leopards in the forest. The deer could well be running for its life with the leopard not too far behind. I quickly looked all around. Taking Aashu's hands in mine, I hastened our pace towards the site.

"Sir, you like the forests… the forests?" Atul was waiting for us patiently.

'Yes, it was lovely, Atul. We feel this site is quite suitable and we can do the deal. What about the land titles and papers? And the price?" I did not want to waste much time.

"Sir, I will give all the papers… all the papers. I think they are all in order but you should get your best lawyers to check them fully and get them validated…

get them validated. Don't worry about the price... the price. While the landowner has said not less than 1 crore per acre, I am sure we can finalise it at 80 lakhs per acre... per acre."

Aashu looked at me and nodded.

"Atul, looks we can do the deal if the land title papers are in order. I will have my lawyers contact you soon. And thank you so much for your cooperation. We should meet up in Delhi sometime soon. It will be our pleasure," I said, shaking hands with Atul.

"Sir, if I can be of use to you and be able to help you... help you, then I am near my salvation... my salvation."

35

We were happy to be back in Delhi. In spite of all the heat, the dirt, the crime, the pollution, and the politicians, Delhi was still very close to our hearts. The change of weather through the year brought in a change in moods and clothes too. The dirt and pollution was largely due to all the construction but it also gave us the wide and spacious roads and flyovers and the metro trains. Crime was inevitable in a society where the disparity between the rich and poor was increasing every day. However, there was an ironical silver lining in all this. Synfra's security services business was booming. So, Jasraj never complained about the rising crime in the city. That leaves the politicians. They were also useful as their behaviour, inaction and corrupt practices gave rise to a new generation of youth activists and young educated people who wanted to join politics to change the system.

Aarvee was very happy to see us. He was growing fast – both in height and girth. I held my mother responsible for this.

"If Aarvee does not eat, how will he become strong? He needs milk, butter and ghee for his growing body," my mother would react.

Apart from milk, butter, ghee and Aashu's chicken, rice, vegetables and juices, Aarvee also had his own favourites – Maggi noodles, biscuits, ice-creams, soft drinks, chocolates, and chips. I was not surprised by Aarvee's growth around his waist and belly. My father and I fortunately balanced this to some extent as we forced Aarvee to play a lot of sports. Left to himself, Aarvee would have been happy playing his video games alone. I was also happy that Aashu had gone back to her running and she sometimes made Aarvee run with her.

My father and I often went for a walk in a nearby park. We loved the time we spent together in the greenery of the park, which had a walking track all around it.

"*Papa*, do you miss *baba* sometimes?"

"Yes, definitely, I do. Why do you ask?"

"You and *baba* had strong differences – much more than we had!"

"Ha ha! Yes, we had our differences. You and I were at least able to sort them out at some stage in life. With *baba*, I did not get that opportunity."

"But what was the main reason for your differences, *papa*?"

"Let us just say that for *baba*, his ego, pride, and honour was before family. And for me, my ego, pride, and honour IS my family."

I did not talk more on this topic.

"*Papa*, what is Bhola doing these days?"

"Oh, he was very sad after *baba's* death. He did not want to work with your *chachu*. Finally, I heard he has started his own business dealing in illegal arms and ammunition."

"Really? I wonder if he deals with air guns too!"

Papa looked at me with a surprised look on his face.

I did not talk more on this topic either.

"*Papa*, what is happening between *chachu* and *choti chachi* now?'

"What will happen? Your *chachu* got what he deserved. Your *choti chachi* has hired some good lawyers in Patna, and the case is dragging on. *Chachu* wants to get away with nominal alimony, but she does not trust him and wants a one-time settlement of 10 crores."

"Wow! That's a real big bounty! Does *chachu* really have that kind of money?"

"Yes, your *chachu* has made a lot of money in the last decade. In India, if you don't pay taxes, compromise on quality, exploit the poor, use your muscle power, and bribe the powerful, you can make lots of money. Your *chachu* became an expert in all this. I hear he has more than 15 crores in cash alone at various bank lockers across Bihar and Jharkhand."

I was interested in this topic. *Chachu* and I had maintained a good relationship after that fateful Jamshedpur visit. He never knew how my dream had turned into his nightmare. We talked on the phone sometimes. And I helped him with some business from Synfra in Jharkhand. However, I enjoyed talking to *choti chachi* even more.

Choti chachi became very lonely after *baba's* demise. But she set two important goals to achieve in life. First was to make sure she won the case against *chachu.* She put in all her ancestral money from her parents' side as well as what *baba* gave her to ensure she got the best and most aggressive legal advisors. Second was to build a school for poor children in Dhanbad; she managed to raise funds from various sources for this. I had put her in touch with Jasraj's wife, Rakhi, who was able to help her a lot with funding.

"It's getting late for my gym, *papa*. The driver will take you back to home. I will walk over to the gym and finish my exercises there."

I had recently joined a gym in a 5-star hotel in the neighbourhood as I was a little bored of exercising alone at the gym in my apartment.

I had a great workout that day with much more energy than ever before. I attributed it to the extra number of red blood cells in my body after the trip to Gazaar. I took a steam bath in the gym and changed into a fresh set of clothes, which I always carried in a bag.

As I strolled into the main lobby area, I heard a soft voice coming from behind me.

"Hi Jeetu."

I turned around and saw Anu sitting in front of the hotel shift manager's desk. Yes, it was Anu Grover.

She had lost a lot of weight and was looking as gorgeous and glamorous as ever. She had streaks of gold and purple in her still strong, straight and long hair. Her skin was radiant and her white teeth sparkled as she looked at me and laughed.

"Jeetu, I never expected to find you here of all the places! Looks like you have been working out lately –

bulging biceps and all." She touched my biceps as she said this.

"Hey Anu! How are you? So good to see you again. What are you doing here?" It did feel good at that time.

"I am fine. Travelling all over. Have nine hotel properties now to look after. And no one else but I to take care of it all. I am here for a hotel conference."

"Oh, come on! You must have a battery of capable managers working under you?"

"Yes, but managing these managers takes most of my time. I wish I had someone next to me, somebody equal to me, who would guide me and advise me and help me on all the strategic issues too." She looked at me with piercing eyes and I could understand her insinuation.

"Jeetu, I don't know if you know. But I did get married some time ago to a scoundrel who I had to put in his place. Good men are always in short supply, but interest from a lonely, very rich, intelligent girl is in even shorter supply." She chuckled.

"I have forgotten the past. And I am happy to do business with you and Synfra again. Should we meet over dinner to discuss?" She still did not believe in wasting time.

"I am now working part time only with Synfra. In fact, Aashu and I have decided to do a real estate project in the hills... you know a holiday home category. You will be a potential client for us."

"Oh yeah, Aashu. How is she? This is exciting I am sure. But we could have done so many more exciting things together. Do you want me to help you in any way on this project?" she offered, reluctantly.

"Thanks Anu. Will surely reach out to you if I need help. Which reminds me, maybe you can use the security services of Synfra for all your hotel properties..."

"Done. Not an issue at all. Please ask somebody to get in touch with my security head. At least then, you will have dinner with me someday. I have to leave now for some work outside."

"Sure will do, Anu. I will give you a call soon. Till then, you take care of yourself and keep that smile always."

"Thanks. And you too take care of those biceps. I may not be this slim always. Ha ha!" She left laughing from the main lobby door.

I waited a bit and then went up to the hotel shift manager.

"Excuse me, where is this hotel conference that the lady talking to me is participating in?" I asked the manager.

"Sorry sir, there is no such conference here. But yes, the lady was asking if everyone from the gym had to pass through the main lobby area to go out."

I smiled and shook my head.

36

"Sir, I spent three days with your lawyers in Almora and Nainital getting all the land papers checked... land papers checked. I think they are quite happy... quite happy." It was Atul Katiyal on the phone.

"That's good news, Atul. Why don't you come to Delhi next week and we can talk further?" I wanted to close the deal the next day itself but didn't want to sound too desperate.

Atul came to Delhi the next week as agreed. Aashu invited him for lunch. She cooked her special mutton *biryani* after marinating the mutton overnight in a mixture of crushed papayas and curd. *Dadu* was also staying with us at that time and he loved mutton *biryani*.

"Ma'am, this is so delicious... so delicious. Reminds me of the mutton *biryani* that my mother used to cook for me... cook for me." Tears welled up in Atul's eyes.

"Oh Atul, thank you and you are most welcome to have my mutton *biryani* anytime you want to." Once Aashu liked someone, she left no stone unturned to make the person happy and comfortable.

"Are you sure you don't want to try the French red wine that *dadu* got for us?" I asked Atul.

"No sir, I never have any form of alcohol... of alcohol," Atul said, waving his hands.

"See! I told you Jeetu that your theory of alcohol and distant cousin and all that does not work with everybody. There are still sane people in this world who don't need alcohol's company to celebrate a success or forget a failure."

I decided in my mind not to have Aashu anywhere near me when I negotiated the final price of the land with Atul.

"So *dadu* sir, you are here on some business work... business work?" Atul asked *dadu*.

"Yes, there is some clearance I needed from the environment department, and I have been running for months for it. This India is only fit for the corrupt and the scoundrels." *Dadu* had been very worried about this clearance as it was affecting his business, and now his health. Aashu was very concerned about it too.

"Sir, I will take you personally to the department tomorrow and get the work done... work done. Just hold for a minute please... minute please." Atul reassured him and dialled some number on his mobile phone.

"Tiger *ji*, how are you sir... are you sir?" he asked in a very friendly voice.

The person at the other end talked for some time, as Atul tried to look calm.

"Tiger *ji*, my promise is my honour... my honour. I will get it done very soon... very soon. Just help me with this one thing for the father of my *bhabhi* who is like a mother to me... mother to me." He was almost pleading. He then stood up from the table and finished his conversation in the adjoining room.

"It will be done tomorrow... done tomorrow," he said with a definitive tone.

Dadu came back home the next afternoon with everything done. We had never seen him so happy.

"This man is a magician. Where did you find him?" *Dadu* could not help singing praises of Atul for the next couple of hours.

I checked with my lawyers, and they were completely satisfied with the title and ownership papers and documents for the land. Atul and I met at a restaurant that evening to discuss the commercial structure. He was in a jovial mood.

"You look very happy, Atul."

"Sir, this is what *nirvana* is... *nirvana* is. I helped ma'am and her *dadu*... her *dadu*. I was of some use to them... use to them." He folded his hands, looked upwards, and chanted something.

"Yes, thanks a lot for that, Atul. Now, you have to help me on the pricing of the land. I know you said 80 lakhs - 1 crore per acre, but I don't think I can go beyond 80. And I can pay only 30 per cent at the time of the sale agreement. Not 50 per cent as you had suggested. The balance will be paid in three months after registration." I laid out all the key terms.

"Sir, that will be very difficult... very difficult. But I will try my best... try my best. This deal is very important to me, sir... to me, sir. I will be getting 5 per cent of the total sale value from the landowner, which will allow me to invest in some proper business again... business again."

I liked Atul's honesty and straightforwardness. I could not imagine any broker in Delhi being so upfront about his fee and definitely not if the percentage was so high.

"I will not go back to the landowner immediately... landowner immediately. Let him think we are not that interested... that interested. After a month, I will talk to him and convince him... convince him."

I really liked Atul's approach and his thought of protecting our interest.

"Atul, I will pay you some commission from our side too."

"No, sir... no, sir. I have had food in your house and see *ma'am* like my mother... my mother. I cannot take anything from you... from you. But if the deal happens, then please help me invest my money in some good business... good business."

"I promise, Atul," I said and shook his hands vigorously. I handed him a packet of mutton *biryani* that Aashu had prepared for him again that day.

37

"Do you know who I bumped into at the grocery store today?" Aashu asked me over dinner.

"Must be some damn lucky guy I suppose," I quipped.

"It was your friend Jasraj. I think he was doing some shopping for his home. How cute *na*!"

"Who? Jasraj?"

"Jeetu! I am talking about him buying groceries. Such a big guy but he still has a lot of humility."

Jasraj was indeed a big guy now. His business was expanding rapidly and he was getting well-known in the political and media circles too. I don't know why but many successful businessmen have a fascination for politics or the movie world. Perhaps popularity is the highest in these two fields. And Jasraj had made his money and now wanted popularity. Not too different from the 'power' in my 5 Ps theory. I hoped he was getting *pyaar* in Rakhi.

Rakhi had somehow convinced Jasraj to enter politics. Jasraj joined a leading political party and, not surprisingly, became in charge of fund-raising activities.

When a leading businessman is given such a role, it's with the expectation that he will personally contribute the most.

I had visited Jasraj a couple of weeks ago.

"Hi, Jeetu. Good to see you. I am feeling pretty low."

"That's surprising! You are doing great in business, you have invested in a leading movie production house, and now I hear you are an important person in politics too."

Jasraj had picked up 26 per cent equity in a listed movie production and distribution house.

"Yes, all that looks great to read in the papers. Nothing more. The business is under a lot of financial stress after I invested in this bloody movie thing. And now these politicians want me to contribute or raise a lot of funds for them."

Jasraj had often confided to me matters that he could not discuss with his family members as they would get anxious. He could not discuss these issues with his business peers, colleagues or relatives because, if word got around, the market would start seeing him as weak. I was neither a businessman nor a family member. And I was in no way a threat to him.

"I sometimes feel so depressed with my life. Your life is so much better, Jeetu. I really envy you. By the way, how is your hill real estate project coming along?" said Jasraj.

"It's looking very positive. And I am hopeful of closing the deal in a month," I said excitedly.

"That's great. I hope you will be able to raise your funds better than I have been able to do so far."

Jasraj and I went out later that night for a few drinks in a newly opened night club. As usual, there were a lot of beautiful girls out there. Many of them recognised Jasraj; they would have done anything to spend some time with him.

"You know, I could have any of these girls. But I will never. You know why? Because I have two very special ladies in my heart. There is no place for anyone else." Jasraj was a little intoxicated after the third glass of red wine.

"Two very special ladies, Jasraj?" I was a bit puzzled.

"Oh, don't focus on that. Focus on my predicament. I have options but I can't exercise those options. I have wealth but no money for the fame I am seeking. I never get what I seek by being a good person. Why should I not turn into a bad person, Jeetu?"

Jasraj had finished his fourth glass by now.

"Because *karma* will take care of your good deeds and your bad deeds." I knew he did not like such discussions.

"Oh, by the way, I met Anu recently. She was looking real hot I must say." I tried to change the subject.

"Really? Anu? I don't like that girl at all. But I think you both would make a great pair."

I was taken aback by Jasraj's suggestion.

Later that night, I wondered again about what Jasraj had said. A few years ago, he was happy that I had kept my distance from Anu. What had changed now? I concluded he was not drunk then and totally sloshed now.

"You know we should call Jasraj and Rakhi over to our house some time. We have never really invited them over for a meal or something." Aashu insisted, after she had met Jasraj at the grocery store.

"Sure, let us do that when Ramky is here next week. It will be good for Jasraj to meet Ramky," I replied.

I was so excited that Ramky was coming to India after such a long gap. Over the past few years, he had set up his own private equity fund and had raised more than a billion dollars. He had made some very smart investments in Mexico and Indonesia, and was always in the lookout for attractive deals. He was also recently featured in the cover story of *Forbes* magazine. I had noticed Atul reading the magazine issue while he was waiting for me in the restaurant where we had our last meeting. I had not told him that I knew Ramky because I feared he would hike the land price.

Ramky had not married. But he took great care of his old parents who stayed half the time with him in the US. Ramky was a risk-taker. His appetite for risks combined with his brains made for an unbeatable combination. I believe he would not have been so successful had he married. Marriage dampens the risk appetite of an individual. You start to think about your family, your children, and the impact of your risky bets on them. Ramky was a fearless crusader. Ramky had always remained in touch with us. Aashu and Ramky got along like a house on fire.

Aashu made several dishes for the dinner with Ramky, Jasraj and Rakhi. *Palak paneer* and *malai kofta* for those who did not have meat. And prawn curry and lamb *keema* for those who enjoyed flesh and blood. Ramky was completely bowled over by Aashu's cooking.

"Aashu, if you ever set up your restaurant, let me know. I will be the first one to invest in it!" I was sure Ramky would have done that.

"Yes, the food is as lovely as Aashu *ji* herself," Jasraj joined in with his compliments.

I could see Aashu blush a little.

"Jeetu, hope you helped her in the cooking," Rakhi enquired. I don't know if women wanted to ensure equality of men and women or just felt insecure and competitive.

"Oh yes, I was as usual her inspiration during cooking. I kept her in a happy mood while she cooked, and as you know a happy hand does happy cooking to make others eat happily!"

We all laughed and sat down for some desserts in the living room. Over dessert, Ramky talked about his new initiative.

"Jeetu, did I tell you about my new social initiative? I have set aside some funds for helping the well-intentioned political parties in emerging economies. See, if I invest in right politics and the parties make the right policies, then my investments are nothing more than taking them out for a lavish dinner in New York!"

Jasraj was visibly excited. He and Ramky had met for the first time and had hit it off well.

"I think Jeetu, I shall start believing in your *karma* theories now. I did the good deed of coming here today and *karma* is rewarding me," said Jasraj.

Ramky agreed to become a large contributor to Jasraj's political fund. Jasraj was very thankful to me for helping him out.

"Oh, I was nothing but a messenger of *karma*," I said and we both laughed.

38

The next day was the Holi festival. Though Ramky had to go to Mumbai for a business meeting, we insisted that he spend the festival with us. Holi was the most important festival in our family.

During Holi, I had seen *baba* smeared in red, green, and yellow colours with the local drum *dhak* hanging around his neck. He would walk with his entourage around the village and sing local folk songs while some of the women joined the dance steps of the men. In the evening, *baba* would prepare *bhang*, a delicious cocktail of milk, finely minced dry fruits, water melon seeds, saffron, rose petals, and powder or paste of dry crushed leaves from the bushes of cannabis. *Bhang* is perhaps the only drink with strong traces of prohibited drugs that is legal and allowed in India, at least during Holi. It's supposed to be an offering to Lord Shiva, and anything remotely related to the gods cannot be illegal in India.

I have seen my father too carry on the tradition of Holi in Jamshedpur. He would buy large tins of industrial silver and gold paint, and then paint everybody methodically in parallel streaks of gold and silver on all the visible parts of the body. This was one festival where the men were allowed to touch the women. Most of the men kept a clear heart and mind while applying colours or paints on the women. But adolescents like us waited for Holi to get that momentary thrill of the physical touch of a woman's body.

I took great pleasure in carrying forward this tradition. Every year on Holi, Aashu would prepare food from morning, while I made *bhang*. Aarvee too joined in with his water balloons. Often my parents came over during Holi and joined in the preparations. This year they could not make it as they had a wedding to attend in Jamshedpur.

I was wearing a white *kurta pyjama* and Aashu was wearing a white *salwar kurta*. Ramky could not stop clicking photographs of us together. He was not very fond of Holi at IIT, as he had slept through one full day and missed classes after having consumed two glasses of *bhang*. But he seemed to have forgotten that. Or he was deliberately trying to forget it and enjoy the festivities with a fresh mind.

A fresh mind is the feeding ground of *bhang*. It slowly surrounds the perimeter of the mind, and then starts closing in from all sides, till the whole mind is filled with *bhang*. At that moment, the *bhang* turns into a form of helium gas and starts to rise slowly. As it rises, it takes the mind upwards. And this feeling can be scary for some.

The trick to counter the attack is to build a strong fence of determination around the perimeter of the mind.

The other interesting feature of *bhang* is its ability to simulate a 'do loop' computer program in the mind. This program repeats an action several times through the control levers of the mind. So if you start laughing, you laugh, laugh and laugh. And if you start crying, you continue to cry. Also funnily, the stop lever of the mind, under the spell of the program, goes into a slow motion mode. So, when your mind lever stops laughing and activates the stop lever to retract that wide smile back to its normal position, it takes 10 times the time compared to the normal time. This leads to an embarrassing situation for the person inflicted with this program to be sitting in a room where he stopped laughing two minutes ago, but he still carries a wide smile on his face.

Ramky and I were going through a combined attack of the 'helium gas effect' and the 'do loop' program. Aashu was sitting in the corner of the room and laughing hysterically. Maybe she was under the spell too.

"Jeetu, don't fly away from me," Ramky said and tried to grab me. He would then let go of me and then repeat the same action after two minutes. I was just glad there was no drain in front of us this time.

Later in the afternoon, we went downstairs to our condominium garden where a rain dance was organised by the apartment society. There were three distinct clusters on the dance floor. The men's cluster, the women's cluster, and the children's cluster. And behind them all was the cool looking DJ who was playing the latest Bollywood songs at full blast.

Ramky got immersed in the men's group very quickly. Aashu and I went up to the DJ and asked him to play an Amitabh Bachchan song which when translated meant "after a bath in the ocean, you become saltier". When the song started playing, Aashu and I went to the centre of the dance area and started to dance in wild abandon. The next song was the mother of all Holi songs. The *rang barse* song from another movie of Amitabh Bachchan, sung by the man himself in his baritone. Aashu tied her white *dupatta* around her waist while I unbuttoned my *kurta*. I then squatted on the ground, while Aashu danced around me. I too danced from waist up, mostly just moving my hands. Aashu, on the other hand, looked like a complete dancing diva.

Ramky and Aarvee stood in the crowd cheering us. I could see Aarvee clapping his hands with innocent glee. Ramky was clicking pictures but I was not sure if he was clicking us or the beautiful women around us.

Suddenly, our dance transitioned into slow motion, and I could see Anu watching me from behind a small gap in the crowd. I shook my head, drank another glass of *bhang* handed to me by Ramky, and I could no longer see Anu. I must add another impact of *bhang* to my research list, I thought – it can translate the sub-conscious thought into momentary reality.

The DJ declared us the best dance couple. We proudly accepted the award and bowed to a cheering crowd. Ramky shouted at the top of his voice, "They deserve the best couple award, not just best dance couple. It's not just their dance that's attractive, it's also their romance." The crowd cheered and clapped again.

It was late evening by the time we washed up and changed into new clothes. We assembled in the living room for some post *bhang* chit-chat. The impact of the *bhang* lasts for at least 12 hours. So we had the necessary stimulant in our bodies for a discussion that I had been wanting to have with Ramky for long.

"Ramky, I have been experiencing a strange phenomenon. I sometimes get dreams that I remember when I wake up. And the dreams come true in a short period of time. I saw my *baba's* exact date of death and Tendulkar scoring a century in a Test match, and many more such incidents. How can I, as an IITian, believe in any of this?"

"Jeetu, this happens to a few people whose subconscious mind or unconscious part of the brain is very strong. And dreams are but the unconscious parts of the brain. There have also been controlled experiments in laboratories in which a person knows when a scary picture will come on the computer screen and when an ordinary picture will appear. The body knows before the mind. Or in your words, *karma* knows what the mind or the body does not."

Ramky was still brilliant in his analysis.

"But why do I see mostly bad dreams? And also, why do I not see incidents of the past?" I pressed further.

"This ability is probably another of our evolutionary strengths for survival. You see premonitions of potential threats or bad events so that you can prepare for them and improve your chances of survival. And for the same reason, you do not see events of the past usually, because they are no longer threats to you."

The *bhang* could not ever enter into the core sanctum of Ramky's gifted brain.

"That seems to make a lot of sense I think," said Aashu.

Ramky excused himself to take a flight to Mumbai. Aashu and I retired to our bedroom to take the flight of passion. Aashu was tired after the day's activities and requested me to press her legs. I obliged happily. I must have been pressing her legs for half an hour at least. Then I said, "Aashu, it's been five minutes since I started pressing your leg. Shall we move on?" I knew it was going to be a long night and I was ready to make love to her, again and again.

39

My mobile phone rang early Sunday morning. I am an early riser and was doing my meditation when the phone rang. It was from some unknown number. I picked it up nevertheless.

“Sir, this is Atul Katiyal… Atul Katiyal. I am calling from a land line number… land line number.” He sounded very excited.

“Hi Atul. Good to hear from you. What’s the latest?”

“Sir, I think we can close the deal now on your terms… your terms. The landowner has agreed to all the terms… all the e d r half an hour at least terms. It was not easy but I managed it well… managed it well. Only one condition he has sir… has sir. Of the initial advance amount of 12 crores, you will have to pay 3 crores in cash… in cash. And the other condition sir is that once the agreement is made and the advance is paid, then there will be no refund in any circumstance… any circumstance.”

“I am okay with it in concept. But I don’t know where I will get this cash in such a short time. I don’t know if I can commit to that part. And I will get the final registration done only when I have got the full in-principle approval and clearance from the authorities for our project."

"Sir, don't worry about that cash part... that cash part. I am sure you will have other investor partners with you... with you. I will arrange for one partner who will bring in about 1 crore in cheque plus the cash part also... cash part also."

"If the partner is good, then I am happy to look at it, Atul. Solves a large part of my problem. Maybe you can come in next week and introduce me to this partner. In the meantime, I will try and secure the balance funds."

This was getting real now. I woke up Aashu and told her about the situation. The total transaction value was going to be Rs 40 crore. We had talked to a financial institution earlier in the month and it had assured to give us Rs 16 crore at an attractive interest rate if we mortgaged the full land and gave a personal guarantee.

I decided to put in about Rs 8 crore of our own savings into the project. If Rs 4 crore came from this friend of Atul, then it left us with a gap of Rs 12 crore.

"Aashu, the three people I know well and would be happy to invest in the project are Jasraj, Ramky, and *chachu*. And they can all chip in about 4 crores each easily."

It was looking feasible and practical to me now.

Over the next couple of days, I made calls to the three of them. Ramky did not ask a single question and said, "I am embarrassed you are asking me for such a small amount, Jeetu." Jasraj asked a couple of questions. "Have you checked the land papers? Do you have a reliable broker?" And then agreed to his share of the equity commitment. He probably saw this as an opportunity to show his appreciation to me for helping him out in the political funding.

I then called *chachu*.

"*Pranaam chachu*! How are you doing? Heard business is doing very well."

"Oh, hello Jeetu and my blessings to you son. You have called after a long time. All well I hope."

'Yes, *chachu*. All well. You know Aashu and I have decided to do a real estate development project in the Uttaranchal hills. And we have identified a great piece of land. I am thinking of having 3-4 partners with me in the project. And who better than you I thought."

"You are a smart guy. And you will always make a smart investment. I am more than happy to back you. After all, you had helped me in my business in the early days. Now, it's my time to help you. How much do you need?" *chachu* asked.

"Total of 4 crores. But initially for the advance, I need maybe 1-2 crores only."

"I have 2 crores lying in the bank and earning some shamefully low interest rate. I will transfer this amount as soon as you confirm. The balance whenever you say."

I was very happy with *chachu's* response. Family after all is family. I felt a slight tinge of guilt remembering the separation of *chachu* and *choti chachi*. Values are values, and families are families. And I decided not to mix them.

I was now looking forward to meeting Atul's friend in the coming week.

Atul informed me that the meeting with his friend was confirmed at the coffee shop of Maurya Sheraton hotel on Tuesday night. I decided to go alone to this meeting even though Aashu wanted to meet the potential partner.

I was greeted in the lobby of the hotel by Atul, and he escorted me to the table where his friend was already waiting.

"Sir, meet Tiger Mahajan or Tiger *ji*...Tiger *ji*. And Tiger *ji*, this is my dear friend Jeetu *ji*... Jeetu *ji*."

"Hi Tiger. Good to meet you." I extended my hands for a shake.

"Jeetu, my dear Jeetu, I have heard so much about you," said Tiger embracing me, much to my embarrassment.

Tiger Mahajan was a tall lanky man in his mid-fifties. He had a very prominent and well-oiled handlebar moustache with the end points very well defined and strongly curving upwards. His face was thin. He had jet black, wavy, long hair, parted from the middle and resting on his narrow shoulders. His face was very fair and slightly wrinkled below the eyes. He looked like a mix of a rock star and an army general.

"It's a pleasure indeed to meet you too, Tiger. Atul has only praises for you."

I considered Atul a good friend now and I had asked him about Tiger's background. Tiger Mahajan was the son of a very powerful politician who had died in a plane accident about 20 years ago. Tiger had studied architecture and had established his own practice after working for a few years in London. He was very successful in his practice; some of the iconic buildings in Delhi were designed by him. He had a son who had joined an undergraduate course in New York in the year 2000. On the fateful day in September 2001, Tiger Mahajan had asked his son to deliver a Ganesha idol as a gift to one of Tiger's clients who had an office in Twin Towers. His son was never found after the attacks.

That incident completely changed Tiger. He sold his practice and went into solitude for almost a year. His wife divorced him shortly and married a widower who was earlier working as the head of finance at Tiger's architecture practice.

Tiger returned from his self-imposed exile with a new appearance. He had nothing more in life to look forward to. He bore a deep-rooted angst against all of humanity. He could not look at a Ganesha idol or photograph. He perspired even if he spotted the deity by accident.

Tiger had set himself a new mission in life. To make as much money as possible in any way possible, wearing the garb of the most friendly and helpful person on earth. He donated most of the money he made to an NGO which was founded primarily for the protection of elephants from poachers who hunted them for ivory tusks. I could not understand why anyone would have such a complicated mission in life, and even if he did, why would he share it with Atul? Perhaps, this was Tiger's way of getting back at Lord Ganesha whom he still held responsible for the death of his son.

Tiger had strong networks in the bureaucratic and political circles of Delhi. He soon rose to be one of the most accomplished wheeler-dealers in Delhi.

He could get anything or anybody fixed for a price. Apparently, Atul had helped him in one of his deals at the government department where Atul's father used to work. And they had become friends since then.

I was a little hesitant at first in making such a powerful person a financial partner in our project. But need is the mother of all greed. And after meeting Tiger, I was assured that he was a nice person at heart who had faced some misfortunes in life.

We discussed the terms of the deal. He agreed to put in Rs 1 crore in cheque and Rs 3 crore in cash for the advance money. He would get 20 per cent equity in the project, even though on paper he was committing far less than the other three partners, Chachu, Jasraj, and Ramky, who held only 15 per cent each. I would hold the balance 35 per cent equity.

I had the money to make the advance payment – Rs 4 crore from Tiger, Rs 4 crore from our savings, Rs 2 crore from Chachu, and Rs 1 crore each from Jasraj and Ramky. The balance amount was also committed to by the same partners. I was in a happy mood. And Tiger could see that.

"Jeetu, I like the fact that you are happy now. But you know happiness never lasts for long. So, you should enjoy the phase while it lasts," said Tiger, patting me on the back while we toasted a drink to seal our verbal agreement.

40

"You won't believe who I met near Aarvee's school today when I had gone to attend the parent-teacher meeting," Aashu said excitedly. I was feeling a bit guilty for not having gone with Aashu to the PTA meeting. But I was so busy finalising the paperwork for our real estate project. And all this would eventually benefit Aarvee only, I thought. Even an educated person like me finds such old school logic handy at times.

"Who Aashu?"

"Jasraj! Imagine bumping into him again!"

Yes, it was a bit odd. What could Jasraj be doing there, I wondered.

"He said he was there to pick up Rakhi's nephew who has joined the nursery class this year," Aashu clarified, as if she had read my mind.

But why would Jasraj come all the way from the city to pick his nephew from a school in Gurgaon? Maybe there was some family function in Gurgaon and Rakhi may have requested Jasraj to pick up her nephew.

"That's nice of Jasraj. Hey Aashu, can you come here please and sign on all these papers?"

There was a lot of hectic activity since the time I met Tiger and secured the funds. I had to form a company, get the shareholder's agreements signed by all partners, get a board approval in place for signing the sale agreement for the land, open a bank account, get the funds transferred into it, and take care of several smaller tasks.

Finally, the day arrived for us to meet the landowner and sign the agreement and pay the advance. We decided to do it in the most auspicious place we knew – our home. The landowner had flown in to Delhi that morning. He was a nice and simple person. Our lawyers had already checked the sale agreement, we had to just sign on the papers.

"Sir, please sign here… sign here. And then ma'am will sign below your signature… your signature," said Atul, pointing at the papers.

"No, I want Aashu to sign first, and I will sign below her signature. It was her dream, her inspiration to do this project, and she deserves to get the higher platform," I said. I looked at Aashu and winked.

We signed the papers and handed a copy to the landowner. We kept a copy for ourselves. Aashu took out some *laddoos* from a box and offered them to everybody as a symbol of a good start.

"Ma'am, just *laddoos* today… *laddoos* today? No mutton *biryani*… mutton *biryani*?" Atul asked, smiling at Aashu.

"Ha, ha. We shall celebrate with *biryani* when we pay the balance amount and get the land finally registered. But as our special friend, you can come home and have *biryani* any time you want."

Aashu was genuinely fond of Atul.

Atul had brought Rs 3 crore in cash from Tiger. He counted and handed the notes to the landowner in front of us.

"Thank you," said the landowner and left.

Aashu waited for the landowner to leave and then he said, "Thank you Atul – you have been a real help to us. How can we ever repay you?"

"With just some more of your mutton *biryani,* ma'am… mutton *biryani*, ma'am."

That night I had a dream where I saw Tiger and Atul exchanging a bag full of cash. I was surprised that I had a dream about an event that had already occurred. Ramky was not always correct in his analysis. Maybe my dreams not only predicted the threats of the future but also recapped the positive developments of the past to take on the threats of the future.

I called Jasraj after a week to inform him about the sale agreement and the advance paid.

"I am really glad this thing is taking off now. I will try and expedite the documentation with the financial institution so that we can give the balance payment at the earliest and register the land," I told Jasraj.

"Great going! I am also looking forward to it. Who is going to help with you the registration work in the hills? That can be a cumbersome task sometimes," Jasraj enquired.

"Oh, it will be taken care of. I have a good friend, Atul, who is helping us in this deal. Atul Katiyal."

"What? Atul Katiyal is your advisor for the land? That dark guy with pimples? How could you do this,

Jeetu? You should have first checked with me at least." Jasraj was terribly upset.

"Atul Katiyal is a first-rate con artist. He has cheated my friend of several crores in the past on the pretext of getting him a negotiated contract for an irrigation project in Uttaranchal through his political links. My friend paid him the cash advance. And Atul disappeared after that from Delhi. My friend could not go to the police because of the sensitive nature of the contract. He is still searching for Atul. Atul's former brother-in-law works at Synfra and, according to him, Atul has been hiding in Haldwani for some time now," Jasraj continued.

I had a sinking feel in my heart. It was as though my heart suddenly became weak and the other organs of the body were pressing it with force. It's the feeling one gets when coming down a rollercoaster ride. I could visualise the downward journey. I wanted to throw up. I wanted to shout. I wanted to cry. But then, I thought, maybe Atul was not a bad person after all, and Jasraj's friend could have had a one-off misunderstanding. Hope was the only way to keep me sane at that moment.

"Atul was never married but…," I stammered.

"Atul was married to a local Punjabi girl from Karol Bagh. She soon realised that she had made a big mistake. She settled for an immediate divorce with no alimony also. Atul had no money in any case as he had squandered away all his money in gambling and drinking." This was getting worse.

"But I had checked with one of Aashu's colleagues who had gone to FMS around the same time as Atul had. And she had confirmed that Atul was from FMS and was a rather shy student there." I was fighting with the last remnants of hope.

"Yes, he did go to FMS and also worked for a few years. He was a smart person I hear. And he did well too and earned a lot money. But then he fell into the gambling and drinking habit and never recovered from there. Why don't you call up his ex-brother-in-law and get more information?" Jasraj suggested.

Jasraj gave me the number of this person and I called him up immediately.

"Hi, I am Jeetu Singh here."

"Oh, hello sir, how are you?"

"Jasraj just told me about this Atul Katiyal who was related to you earlier. I have just done a deal through him, and I am very concerned…"

"Sir, what have you done? Atul Katiyal is a scoundrel. He has cheated so many innocent people. He cheated my sister too. All he is concerned about is playing with people's emotions, gambling and drinking, and worrying about his big pimples! But he is very smart and gets away always because there is no documentary evidence. But I know the person with whom he is hiding in Haldwani, and I can get some information for you if you want," he said, offering to help.

"That would be a great help indeed."

I did not immediately inform Aashu. I wanted to find out more, and I was still hopeful. I tried to call Atul Katiyal on his mobile phone a few times but I got the same message every time, 'This number is temporarily disconnected.' I knew intuitively that life was not going to be the same now. I was disconnected from my faith in humanity.

41

I was restless the whole night. Aashu could sense that something was amiss. When she saw me tossing in bed around 2 a.m., she got up and came close to me. Without saying anything, she rested my head on her lap and caressed my hair lightly. She did this for the next three hours I think because I was woken up at 5 a.m. by the alarm.

I looked up at her, and she was smiling. She looked fresh, as though she had just had a bath. I could not look her into the eyes directly. She asked nothing and just said, "Remember, whatever happens, I am there with you in this life and all your future lives."

For the next couple of days, I tried to spend as much time as possible outside the house. I had a few close friends from school living in Delhi, and I went to them and narrated the incident. They were all very supportive and sympathetic. And they kept asking me more and more about Atul and how it had come to this. How could an intelligent person like me fall for such a con artist? I was sure my friends were feeling bad for me, but I also knew they were relieved that they had not fallen into such a trap. Feeding on the misfortunes and miseries of others is a subconscious way of the mind keeping itself healthy. The outer bodies of my friends would not feed on this misfortune but their minds were constructed to do so and I did not blame them for it.

That night walking into my condominium, I could see wild animals lurking behind the manicured bushes surrounding the boundary walls. I could see red horns coming out of the heads of the security guards standing at the entrance of the tower lobby. I could feel my own face mocking me in the mirrors of the elevator leading up to my apartment. When I rang the doorbell of my apartment, I was startled by the noise it made. When Aashu opened the door, I was shivering.

"Where have you been all day?" She was visibly upset and concerned.

I just went inside and collapsed in the sofa in the living room. I heard my mobile phone ringing, and saw an unknown number. Could it be Atul? I rushed to pick it up.

"Sir, I don't have good news for you." It was Atul's former brother-in-law.

"Tell me everything," I said, in a soft whisper. My voice had lost its strength too.

"Sir, the land you have purchased is actually going to be notified very soon as a forest land. The landowner and Atul were aware of this. Atul had made a deal with the landowner to keep all the cash advance himself; he would also get 50 per cent of the cheque money that the landowner received. The landowner was supposed to transfer the money into Atul's offshore account. He has probably done that already. And Atul has left Haldwani and cannot be traced."

I could not hold the phone any longer and put it down. I lay down on the sofa again, staring at the ceiling. I was happy that there was no fan on the ceiling as my suicidal thoughts were overpowering me that instant. I tried to divert my mind and retraced some of the events. The papers that Atul had showed me when I had expressed concern about the forests nearby were obviously forged. Hence, he had not given them to me. His chants and prayers for salvation were all humbug. He had helped *dadu* to win Aashu's confidence. Everything about the timing and the payment terms suited him perfectly. He knew that we would not get the land registered, and hence decided to flee with whatever he had. I had no basis to make a formal police complaint. I was left with no option but to pull back from the project and lose all the money paid so far.

I had lost a large part of my hard-earned money. Money on which I had paid full tax to the government. Money for which I had stayed away from my family for so many days travelling. Money for which I had put my health at risk. To lose a large part of that to a cheat, a gambler, and an alcoholic was akin to the pain from a poisonous snake biting me every 10 minutes.

I decided that Aashu should not be disturbed during this period. Aarvee needed her. I needed her. Aarvee was on his summer vacation holidays and I decided to send them both to Kolkata to Aashu's parents place. I wanted to deal with this myself. I knew I would feel weak and miserable at night and miss Aashu a lot. But at least during the day time, I wanted the courage to fight without the fear of something happening to my family at home.

Next morning at the airport, as I dropped them off, Aashu kissed me on the forehead and said softly, "Jeetu, remember that tough times do not last. Tough people do." She had the impression that my deal with the financial institution had fallen through and I made no efforts to clarify her false assumption.

Jasraj and Ramky were very supportive and they genuinely felt very sorry for me. They encouraged me not to worry about it too much. "Don't burn your good blood over that scoundrel's bad blood," Jasraj said and then added, "In case you and Aashu want to return to full-time work again, then Synfra's door will always be open."

Ramky had only this to say, "Let's forGIVE him but GIVE him his due first. Let's forGET him – but let him GET what he deserves first." I knew Ramky was serious about it.

I called up *chachu* soon after talking to Jasraj and Ramky.

"*Chachu,* we may have lost our initial investment in the land. There won't be any meaningful development allowed on that land. I was misled by the broker."

"What? How can this be, Jeetu? You are supposed to be from the industry. You should have known all this before taking money from me." *Chachu's* voice was stern.

"Well, as I said, I was shown forged papers and all. It's good we paid only 30 per cent advance otherwise we could have lost the whole amount, *chachu,*" I tried to reason with him.

"That's no consolation for me. I have lost 2 crores. Who will pay for that? Do you know how much trouble

I had to go through to earn 2 crores? And you tell me now that it's all gone in a second! I trusted you, you should have taken care of my investment." *Chachu's* voice was getting louder and louder.

"But *chachu*, we all signed the agreements, and we all knew there was some risk as equity partners. There was no guarantee from me to anybody."

"I don't know about all this. I gave you money on the expectation of a good return on my money. You have to make sure you give at least my principal amount back. Out here in Jharkhand, you know what we do to people who don't return our money? Next time call me when you have the money with you or you better take care of your family and not let them come to Jharkhand again." *Chachu's* threat was quite blunt and he did not disguise it any way.

Blood is thicker than water but blood evaporates rapidly before the scent of money. I had never imagined *chachu* to react this way. Maybe when you lose your own family, you don't want any other family to remain happy. And money remains your sole hope for old age and troubled times. I was sure *baba* would have pointed his double-barrelled Ichhapur manufactured gun at *chachu* from the heavens high above.

42

"Jeetu, my man! How are you doing? You seem to have forgotten me!" Tiger Mahajan was on the phone.

"Hi Tiger. I was thinking of calling you myself. Can we meet sometime soon?"

"Why not? I am always happy to meet smart young fellows like you. I am in Gurgaon this afternoon for a meeting. Maybe we can meet at this new German beer bar at the mall next to your apartment? Say 5 p.m.?"

I was surprised he knew where I lived. I don't remember telling that to him. Must have been that scoundrel Atul.

"Done Tiger. Will see you there."

The bar was on the top floor of the mall and had glass walls on three sides, giving a panoramic view of the golf course. Usually this place was very crowded but we were early guests and the place was nearly vacant other than a group of middle-aged ladies playing kitty. As we crossed this group of women, Tiger bowed a bit and then brushed his long hair backwards with his hand. Tiger was looking dashing in a sports jacket and corduroy trousers. We took a table in the corner from where we had an uninterrupted view of the main road and the golf course.

"Do you play golf, Jeetu?"

"Not much. It's too slow a game for me." I remembered the couple of times I had tried playing with Jasraj but I did not enjoy it much.

"It's a game of the mind. Do you not like mind games, my dear?" He twirled his moustache upwards. He was proud of his mind games on the golf course and outside it.

The waiters and bartenders were very well-dressed and very courteous. We were offered samples of three kinds of freshly brewed beer. We both settled for wheat beer, which had a slightly unusual flavour. I thought the wheat in it must be healthy in some way for me.

"Tiger, there has been a problem with the hill project," I said, having the first sip of the beer.

"Problem? Problems are good, my friend. They make you feel like a man after you have solved them." Tiger gave another twirl to his moustache.

"Tiger, I don't think we can really develop that project as it's getting notified under the forest area. And there is no point in getting the land now. But as per our agreements, we cannot have the refund of the advance amount now. As your equity share was 20 per cent, you should get back the additional 160 lakhs you had paid for the advance. I hope you will agree that's fair," I said with a straight face.

"Fair? Life is not fair. It's never been fair to me, my friend! I want my full 4 crores back and not a single rupee less!" Tiger's eyes shrunk as he gulped down half the glass in one shot.

"The only concession I can give you is that you can give me the full amount in cheque. I can understand you will not have that much cash with you, otherwise you would not have approached me in the first place. I can be a considerate man Jeetu as long as you don't play mind games with me. I hate losing on the golf course, and I have never lost outside it since the time I lost my son and my marriage!"

So Atul was right for once, I thought.

"But Tiger, I have lost so much of my own money already, and we all were in it as equity partners." I tried to convince him.

"There is no permanent partnership in life. Not with your wife, not with your children. It's all a matter of convenience. It was convenient for you to include me as a partner to get the cash. And now the only thing convenient for me is to get my full principal amount back." Tiger was in no mood to listen.

"Let me also advise you Jeetu that my name is not Tiger for nothing. I can hunt down my prey when I want to." Tiger had finished his second glass of beer by now and didn't hesitate to threaten me outright.

"I will wait to hear from you," said Tiger, drinking his third glass in one gulp. He then got up, embraced me tightly, and whispered in my ears, "Start playing golf, my friend. There are only snakes to fear in the greens, not tigers."

He left and I took care of the payments hurriedly.

Ramky and Jasraj were happy to pool in and pay off Tiger Mahajan. But I was completely against it. *Baba* would have been ashamed of me if I buckled under such threats and did not follow what was fair and just in my mind and heart.

"There is no greater threat than the threat of living the rest of your life with the feeling that fear got the better of what was fair," *baba* would sometimes tell me.

I was no longer a *goonda* like I had been in my youth, but I was no pushover either. My body may have weakened but my mind had gotten stronger. My only weakness was my family. But my family, and Aashu definitely, would also want me to do what is fair and just. I decided to do what was fair.

I sent a text message to Tiger the next day.

'Tiger, I can pay you what is fair and as I had committed. Please do not expect anything more. I know a tiger can hunt. But remember that even a child can throw a stone at a tiger in the cage.'

I was not sure what I wanted to convey but it felt good typing this.

I did not hear back from Tiger for a couple of days. On the third day, at 4.30 a.m., I heard the door bell ringing incessantly. I dragged myself to the door and opened it. I saw Tiger standing there with two tall burly men who looked like the bouncers I had seen in many bars. Tiger was outside its cage and ready to hunt.

"Jeetu, did I wake you up my friend? I am so sorry. I was in a party at the nearby 5-star hotel till early this morning, and then I saw this lovely cake in the bakery as I was leaving. I could not resist buying it for your family. Here, please have it and extend my best wishes to your lovely wife and son." He handed the packet to me and left.

I opened the packet with a bit of caution, and was relieved to find it was actually a cake. A cake made in the shape and colours of a tiger with long white chocolate pieces for the front and back teeth. I took those chocolate pieces first, broke them into two halves, and popped them in my mouth. They were delicious.

I got a couple of security guards from Synfra to watch my apartment round the clock.

43

'Thank you for the lovely cake.' I sent a text message to Tiger. I also added a photo of Ganesha after the message. I got no reply to it.

I got no call or message for the next few days. The following Monday, I had to go to Nehru Place for a meeting with my lawyer in the afternoon. It was a very dusty day; there were dust winds blinding most parts of Delhi for about half an hour. Some said the dust wind had originated from the deserts of Rajasthan and then travelled to Delhi. I was lucky to be inside my lawyer's office during that time. When I came out, my driver, as usual, was sitting in the front seat and listening to some local songs on his headphone. He stepped out and opened the door for me. It was then I noticed a drawing on the glass window. It was quite visible because of the dust particles in the background. The drawing resembled a tiger. The word TIGER was written below it in capital letters.

As soon as I reached home that evening, I received a call from *chachu* on the land line.

"What is the status? When are you paying my money?" There was no greeting or warmth in his voice at all.

"*Chachu*, why are you behaving this way? I told you the situation clearly. How can you expect me to pay you?" I was quite irritated and it showed in my voice.

"Look Jeetu, if you can't pay, then you should sign your share of the ancestral home in the village in my name. After all, you are the only son and this property will come to you after your father's death."

I was very angry with *chachu's* suggestion. He was using this one incident to get hold of the ancestral property. I was convinced that passion for a man or woman and greed for property or land were the only two things that changed people and made them commit crimes that they would otherwise have never thought of.

"*Chachu*, if that's what is going to make you happy, so be it. The next time I am in Jharkhand, I shall do so. You can live and die all alone in the big ancestral home!" Saying so, I slammed the phone down.

I was aware *choti chachi* was still living in the ancestral home and would continue to do so unless *chachu* finally settled his divorce with her. I had talked to *choti chachi* the previous week and shared with her in confidence about my transaction with *chachu* and his reactions lately.

I was feeling very depressed that day. I knew I had to remain strong. But the chemicals of the brain work in a different manner. They listen to the body and not the soul. And they secrete substances that cloud the mind and the body with a sense of despair and hopeless gloom. I was missing Aashu a lot that day. I thought of calling her up but she would sense the sadness in my voice and then become sad herself. I just sent her a text message.

'Hi! All well here. Just caught up in meetings and sorting out a few things. Will call soon in a day or so. Love.'

Nothing much happened for the next one week. I assumed that Tiger had probably understood the situation better and was willing to let go of his ludicrous and greedy demand. After a couple of quick and hurried calls to Aashu last week, I finally talked at length that day to Aashu. She was happy to find me a bit relaxed and my voice a bit cheerful. I still had not told her the whole story. I didn't want to tell her anything till she was back in Delhi. "Keep the faith Jeetu. Everything will be all right," Aashu had said, as she reluctantly kept the phone down.

The next couple of calls that day indeed made me introspect deeply into my faith in humanity.

The first call was from my mother.

"Jeetu, there is some good news. *Choti chachi* has finally agreed for a divorce and, more importantly, your *chachu* has agreed to all her terms." My mother had always wanted an amicable settlement and she was clearly happy about the prospect now.

"What did *chachu* agree to?" I was curious to know.

"He agreed to give her a one-time settlement of 4 crores if she left the ancestral house within a period of six months."

Chachu was indeed a shrewd businessman. He knew that the value of the ancestral home was far more than 4 crores and he could now have the whole house to himself.

I had just disconnected the landline phone after talking to my mother when my mobile phone started ringing. It was from Atul's ex-brother-in-law. I had saved his number.

"Sir, I have some very interesting news for you! I came to know from confirmed sources that Atul had taken a loan of Rs 2 crore from some powerful man called Tiger Mahajan. And then he was unable to pay him back. Tiger was after his life. But just a few days ago, Atul went and paid Tiger Mahajan the full 2 crores in cash which he was carrying in a bag!'"

My last dream flashed in front of my eyes again. Atul was actually giving a bag of cash to Tiger and not taking it from him. My dream did try to warn me of the future threat. Ramky was always correct.

44

How could God create people like Atul and Tiger? But then if you did not have people like Atul and Tiger, you will never realise the goodness of people like Jasraj and Ramky. Atul had turned out to be the perfect con artist again for Tiger. He had made Tiger pay 4 crores and from this money he repaid his personal loan to Tiger. Atul had just shifted the monkey from his shoulders to mine. I hoped Tiger would not leave Atul and used his networks to trace Atul and punish him. The thought made me happy in some weird twisted way.

I was also hoping that after getting the cash from Atul, Tiger would have become satisfied with my original offer. Maybe that is why he had been silent for so long. But a leopard never changes its spots and a tiger never lets a prey get away from its jaws, even if it's not hungry.

On a Sunday evening, my personal security guards informed me that there was a lady from Aarvee's school who wanted to see me. I asked them to let the lady in and make her sit in the living room. I changed into something appropriate and then went to the living room and greeted the lady.

"Sir, I work for Tiger Mahajan and he has asked me to give this envelope to you," she said, handing me the envelope. "You can open it later, sir. I will take your leave now."

I was speechless for a while. I opened the envelope with trembling fingers and found a school photograph of Aarvee with all the students in his class. Aarvee was marked in a red circle. Behind the photograph was written in big bold letters: A TIGER ALWAYS HAS HIS 4 MEALS!' The '4' was clearly underlined and obviously referred to the 4 crores he was demanding from me.

I felt weak in my knees and sat down on the sofa. My fingers continued to tremble. I should have just paid Tiger this 4 crores, I thought for a fleeting moment. "You become weaker, and the bully becomes stronger," I remembered *baba's* words. No, I was not going to yield to this bully's demands. I thought of going to the police but then realised I did not have any proof. And Tiger would probably use his influence to get me into more trouble. But Tiger was threatening my family, my blood.

I was prepared to shed blood to protect my blood. But I would take my time and think over it. I just made sure I had Bhola's number on my phone. I did not call Bhola from my phone, but I did call up Aashu and told her to postpone her return by another couple of weeks. She was not pleased about this but Aarvee's holidays had also been extended due to the extreme heat. She thought it might be better for Aarvee to stay in Kolkata, which was experiencing a milder summer that year.

This was probably the lowest point in my life so far. I had sacrificed my career, lost a large part of my savings, committed my ancestral home to *chachu*, was living away from Aashu for such a long period for the first time, and had Tiger hounding me. But I took solace in *baba's* words again. "The saddest part in a movie is just before the best song in the movie." I was not aware though that the song was about to begin soon.

My mobile flashed *chachu's* number. I did not want to pick it up. I had already agreed to what he wanted. What more could he want now?

"Yes, *chachu*?"

"Can I fly over to Delhi and get the paper signed from you tomorrow?" *chachu* asked me in a polite voice this time.

"Hmm... I am not sure what your hurry is, *chachu*. But yes, why not?" I didn't really bother.

"Great! Will see you tomorrow then." He seemed very excited.

The phone rang again. It was from *choti chachi* this time.

"Jeetu, give me your bank account details. I am transferring 2 crores to your account from the 4 crores I received from your *chachu* this morning."

I did not know how to react. But I could understand *chachu's* hurry now.

"No, no, *choti chachi*. That's your money. You should keep it. Don't worry, I will tackled *chachu*," I insisted.

"Jeetu, I will remain unhappy all my life if you refuse. This is *chachu's* money that is going to go back to him. The balance 2 crores will be more than enough for me. The only reason I had settled for this divorce was so that I could help you and feel happy. Don't you want your *choti chachi* to be happy for the rest of her life? If you do, then please do not say another word, and just accept the money. Oh and give me your bank details, of course!"

I remained silent for several seconds. Tears started to roll down my cheeks, and then I said, "Thank you, *choti chachi*. May I be born as your own son in the next life!" I could hear her sobbing silently before she said, "You are my son in this life too." She then kept the phone down. I messaged her my bank details later and within an hour I got a call from my bank manager informing me of Rs 2 crore being credited to my account.

The next day, when *chachu* arrived at my home, I welcomed him and touched his feet for his blessings. He had brought all the papers and documents with him.

"Son, can you just sign at these two places, please?" He was family now again. Our own blood. But contaminated blood.

"*Chachu*, maybe you should look at this first before I sign?" I handed him a Rs 2 crore demand draft from my bank in his name.

His face went blank. His eyes started to twitch. He wanted to say something but could not.

I got up, folded my hands, and said thank you. I then showed him the way to the door.

As I closed the door behind him, I had no idea of the person who would open the door for me exactly a week from then when I returned from my evening jog.

45

"Sir, so good to see you after so many years." Bhola Yadav opened the door for me. He knew the servant at my home and had let himself in about an hour ago. Bhola had not changed much except that he had lost some more hair.

"Bhola! What are you doing here? And why didn't you call me before?" I exclaimed, rubbing the sweat off my forehead after the jog.

"Sir, I was on a private mission here. But I could not go back before seeing you."

"Private mission? You are now Bhola Bond, are you?"

Bhola looked a bit embarrassed.

"Anyway, always good to see you, Bhola. Just let me refresh myself and then we shall maybe have a drink together."

I had never shared a drink with Bhola before but the man deserved a toast for having been so faithful to our family for so long. And a toast is no fun without two glasses clinking together. I sat on the sofa but Bhola simply refused to sit on the same sofa. He sat on the carpeted floor next to the sofa and made himself comfortable there. We toasted our first drink to *baba*. "To the bravest man to have walked this planet!" I had learnt that toasts are always about a bit of melodrama. And it felt good to do this melodrama after all the real life drama in my own life.

Our second toast was "to the bravest doll that stood on top of my head." We both had a good long laugh.

Our third toast was "to the tiger Bhola never got to kill." I remembered Bhola's complaint after *baba* had shot the tiger.

"Sir, I have hunted down my first tiger," Bhola shouted.

"What do you mean, Bhola? When did you do this? Which forest?" I was quite surprised.

"Just this week only, sir. In the bad jungles of your Delhi," Bhola replied with a straight face and slightly intoxicated eyes.

"You want to see the photo of this tiger?" Bhola asked, as he pulled something from the back pocket of his trousers.

"Sir, this was the tiger I had come to hunt in Delhi."

I looked at the photograph. And almost jumped from my seat. It was Tiger Mahajan's photograph.

"This is Tiger Mahajan! Bhola, how are you connected to him? And why were you hunting him?"

"Sir, this Tiger was a large dealer for illegal arms supply to Bihar and Jharkhand. All the mafia and politicians in the two states are his clients. About a year ago, he took an advance of Rs 4 crore from a powerful politician in Dhanbad. You probably know him. Anyway, Tiger Mahajan took this advance but did not deliver the arms. When the politician asked him to pay the money back, he said that he had already paid the money to the arms manufacturer in Russia and had no money with him."

"And then?" I could not wait to hear the full story.

"Then what, sir? The politician got angry and said it is not about the money. It is about his principles, name, ego and pride. So he hired me for a very attractive amount to hunt him down. And here I am today after having hunted him down."

"How did you hunt him, Bhola?" My interest was peaking.

"Sir, it's better that I do not share the finer details with you. Let me just say he will not be seen around. But I had so much fun tracking him down before the final hunt. That I will share with you."

"Go on, go on!"

"I first arrived at his doorstep dressed like Lord Shiva. After all I am Bhola, the other name for Shiva. As he opened the door, I announced that I was Shiva, the father of Ganesha, and that I needed a man's head to replace my son's elephant head."

Bhola was laughing loudly as he said this.

"Sir, you should have seen the look on Tiger's face. He became a cat from a tiger. He just fainted and fell down on the floor. There is no fun in hunting a sleeping tiger, sir. So, I left that day."

I poured some more drink into Bhola's empty glass.

"For the next two days, he did not come out from his house at all. I was, of course, waiting outside his house and keeping a watch on him. You know just like *baba* used to do on a *machan* while waiting for his tiger. Finally, on the third day, he stepped out with a bodyguard by his side. He looked around in fear initially, and when he saw no one around, he twirled that long moustache of his upwards and sat in his car. I followed him in an autorickshaw. He went to a hair salon. The bodyguard waited outside. I then entered the salon from the back door, pointed my silver pistol… you have seen that one *na*… at the two barbers and one other client sitting there."

Bhola was enjoying this narration as much as I was.

"But didn't Tiger see you and react?" I interrupted.

"Sir, Tiger was facing the mirror and his eyes were closed. He was probably thinking about me only. Ha ha! Anyway, listen *na,* sir. Tiger had got his hair cut by then and wanted a barber's shave – you know how smooth it is when a barber shaves. He had shaving foam on his entire face and also a little bit on his moustache. I took the knife from the barber and asked him to step aside. And in one single move, I shaved off his entire moustache, sir. His entire moustache!" Bhola was almost rolling on the floor by now.

"Tiger was shocked but could not shout as I had my knife on his neck by then. I told him I would get more money for cutting his ego and then hunting him down. You see sir, his moustache was his ego. He had hurt my client's ego. And I had to cut his ego. Equal-equal."

"What did you do next?" I was also laughing from inside.

"Sir, I had wounded a tiger. It's so much fun hunting down a wounded tiger. It's more dangerous. *Baba* used to love this. So, what did I do next? I let him go. I started thumping the wooden shelves loudly. You know, in the Chota Nagpur forest, *baba* asked us to carry big drums sometimes to make noises so that the tiger would get nervous and start running around."

This was getting more and more interesting, I thought.

"Sir, but this Tiger went and hid in his cave after that. He did not come out from his house for the next three days. I got worried. I had to find a goat for him now."

"Goat? Why did you have to find a goat for him?" I was puzzled.

"Oh, not that way sir. When *baba* used to hunt, he always carried a goat which he tied to a tree. The tiger would get the scent of the goat and then come out to eat it. And then *dhickchiau*!'" He pointed his fingers like a pistol and took aim at Tiger's photo.

"So, where did you find his goat?"

"Sir, not difficult at all. I know a scrap mafia guy from Jamshedpur who knew Tiger. I had him call Tiger and tell him that he needed guns immediately. And that he would give him an advance of Rs 5 crore immediately that day at Humayun's Tomb."

The goat was perfect, and the tree was perfect too. Humayun's Tomb was an architectural marvel of the Mughal era. I was sure Tiger Mahajan would have studied about it in his architecture course in college.

"The goat served its purpose, sir. And Tiger came. And I had my first Tiger hunt finally!" Bhola declared with a sense of victory.

I did not want to know more. Some things are better left untold. I realised now why Tiger was not hounding me for the past one week. And I also realised that he would never hound me in future too.

46

I woke up with a major hangover from all the drinking the previous night. Bhola was to leave early in the morning. I wondered if he even knew what a hangover was. My hangover gave me a headache but it was a sweet headache. Like the pains you get in different parts of your body, the nerves, and the joints when you are having a massage or when somebody presses with a lot of force at the base of your fingers or toes. I called them 'sweet pain'. They did send the pain signals to the brain but a parallel signal of relief and pleasure was also sent to the brain. My hangover was sending the same parallel signals to my brain. I was in pain but I was also relieved and happy to put the Tiger nightmare behind me.

I had some lime water with honey, and a couple of bananas, which helped me ease the hangover. I was now fully ready to call Aashu. No pain and no fear.

"Hi! Looks like you are enjoying Kolkata so much that you don't miss me at all." I pulled Aashu's leg.

"Yes, I don't miss you Jeetu because I never get separated from you. You are always in my mind and heart, sometimes pleasing me and sometimes troubling me." Aashu did not laugh out aloud like she normally did after saying something like this.

"I know, Aashu. I may have troubled you in the past few days. But I am ready to please you now. Take a flight this evening and come back home."

"Really? All well?" Aashu's voice suddenly perked up.

"Life is good as long as we stay together, eat together, and laugh together. So, everything will be well as soon as you and Aarvee get back home."

I didn't want to get into the details over phone.

"That's superb! I look forward to doing many other things together tonight in the bedroom," Aashu said, in a slightly husky voice. This was enough to get me aroused.

The driver went to pick up Aashu and Aarvee. I decided to stay back and take over the kitchen from my cook. I had to make something different that day. Not my usual brown rice, red beans, and sausage curry. After a lot of deliberation, I settled for noodles with red beans and sausage curry.

The flight was on time for a change and Aashu and Aarvee reached home before 8 p.m. Aarvee had gained some more weight, probably from all the *rosogollas* and *mishti doi* that he loved so much. Aashu had lost some weight, probably thinking and stressing about me.

"Guys! I have cooked a very special dinner for you," I announced pompously.

"Oh no, *papa*. Not again! *Mamma*, we should have stayed back in Kolkata!"

Aarvee clearly had other tastes.

"Jasraj happened to be on the same flight from Kolkata. I told him that I thought he was following me! We both laughed. He was actually in Kolkata with Rakhi for a wedding, and Rakhi had stayed back for a few more days," said Aashu.

I was a little concerned if Jasraj had told her anything.

"Did you two sit together?" I asked Aashu.

"Oh no, he was in business class. We briefly met near the baggage claim area. I was too busy running around Aarvee and collecting my bags. But I was a bit surprised when he wished me goodbye. He said something like, 'Don't worry, Aashu *ji*. We will take care of Atul and Tiger.'"

"Time for dinner, everybody! This is much better than the food you would have had in Kolkata all these days." I changed the subject deliberately.

Aashu poked me lovingly.

For the rest of the dinner, Aashu could not keep her hands off me. She kept touching me, patting me, and tickling me over some pretext or the other. I liked the feel of her touch. I felt alive again. I felt strong again. I can take on a hundred Tigers and *chachus* in this world if I just have my one Aashu.

We hurried through the rest of our dinner, put Aarvee in bed, and headed straight to our bedroom.

Physical separation is sometimes helpful for enhancing the passion in bed. And disentangling yourself from a complex web of troubles can be a stronger enhancement for passion in bed. Together, these enhancers can be a powerful potion for two loving souls. We merged as one powerful force, the kind we had never experienced before.

It was time to share the details of the past few weeks with Aashu. She listened very patiently without saying a single word. At the end of it, she just hugged me tight for what seemed like an eternity.

"It must have been awful. And you had to bear it all yourself! I should have had this pain because I was the one who encouraged you to leave your job and do this project. I would have plucked that Tiger's eyes with my bare hands. How dare he even think of hurting Aarvee?"

We walked out to the balcony with a glass of milk each in our hands. We liked to have a glass of milk at night together. This was a habit I had picked up from Aashu. I often teased her that her skin was milky white due to the gallons of milk she consumed.

It was a clear full moon night. The stars and some of the planets were shining with greater clarity than on most nights. It was still not as clear and bright as the skies in Gazaar but we were now satisfied with the Gurgaon skies. At least it did not dazzle us into blindness.

"You know what, Jeetu? I think your *karma* theory may actually have some meaning. I have been thinking about it for some time. If you look back, Nirupama came to our lives briefly only to create separation between us. Just like you had probably separated her from her boyfriend in the school days?"

"I did not separate anybody! I just fought for my honour." I disagreed strongly.

"Exactly! You are just a small cog in the wheel of *karma*. You don't do things with a particular motive but the outcomes are already defined by *karma*. Nirupama also did not come in our lives with the motive to separate us, did she?"

"You have a point there, Aashu. Maybe the dream I shared with *choti chachi* was planned with the outcome of *choti chachi* eventually helping me in this crisis. And Ramky helping Jasraj actually helped me in this crisis."

"Well, I don't know about Jasraj and Ramky. You have already helped Jasraj a lot in his business, and it was his moral duty to help you out." Aashu went on.

"But what about Ramky? He has been such a help to us and we have never done any help for him." I wondered aloud.

"I feel *karma* works in many ways. Sometimes, it may be repayment of a *karma* from a previous life. Sometimes, you just become a messenger of *karma* without knowing it but it is related to your own *karma* in some way. Like you, Nirupama or *choti chachi*. And sometimes, there are totally different people who are sent in this life with the purpose of hurting you or helping you. And they follow a different *karma* cycle. Like Bhola and Tiger perhaps." Aashu was getting very philosophical now.

"Ha ha! Yes, Bhola was born to help me and protect me from my ill-wishers. But I think Tiger was sent to my life because *baba* killed a tiger." I was enjoying this conversation.

"That may be carrying the logic a bit too far. But yes, who knows? Could be possible. We humans are nothing but chimpanzees when it comes to understanding the ways and science of the grand designer."

I didn't like being compared to a chimpanzee.

"But Jasraj feels there is no evidence of the link between good rewards and good deeds or punishment and bad deeds. He quotes the *Gita* too and says God has asked us to do our deeds. And God will do what he is supposed to. He does not say that you will be rewarded IF you do good deeds." I tried to show higher intelligence than that of a chimpanzee.

"Jasraj is a businessman and wants to justify some of his bad deeds. Ask him if he has any evidence of God. Why believe in God also then? Belief is all we have – in God and in *karma*. And God is God only because he is fair and just." Aashu was completely dismissive of Jasraj's logic.

"One last thing on a serious note, Jeetu. *Karma* also wants you to sometimes take actions directly to close the loop of *karma*. And you must promise me to close this loop with that bastard Atul Katiyal." Aashu held my hand and looked at me.

There are not many times that Aashu requested me for something. I could never refuse her.

"I promise you, Aashu. Atul Katiyal will beg God to be never born again lest he runs into us again. I promise."

We finished our glass of milk and continued to stare at the moon for a long time, holding each other's hands.

47

I had to decide my future career quickly. Over the next few weeks, I started having several discussions with business people I knew and with executive search firms too. But I had to give the first right of refusal to Jasraj. There was no way I could take another job if Jasraj wanted me to work with him again.

"Sure, you are always welcome to come back to Synfra. But I have already made a couple of offers to very senior industry people to join as the CEO and COO. We will have to create some new role for you now because you may not be comfortable working under them," Jasraj said, sitting in his opulent office chair.

"I think it may be difficult then and create more confusion. I will take the other option I have. Recently, Ramky introduced me to a US-based real estate investment fund; it wants to start its India operations and is looking for a Country Head. I have had telephonic and video conferences with their board members, and they have made me an attractive offer."

"That's great news! You should take it up. But in case Aashu *ji* is keen to return to a job, I have the role of a sales and marketing head that she can possibly consider," Jasraj graciously offered.

"Thanks Jasraj. That's really nice of you. Aashu and I have discussed this. And we agreed that I will take up a full-time job again while she takes care of Aarvee's education and health in these critical years. She may do some part-time freelance work from home later."

"Always the sacrificing Aashu *ji*! You must have prayed to some special god to get such a special wife! You must tell me which god it is so that I pray to him for my future." Jasraj laughed loudly.

"Future? You have such a great partner in Rakhi! How can you even think of anyone else?" I said, though I knew he was joking.

"Future can also mean next life, my friend. It was you who taught me about next life and all that," Jasraj said, almost accusingly.

We both laughed together. It was the joy of two friends who cared for each other, sharing a light hearted banter.

I joined the real estate fund Real T the following week. I liked the innovative and unique name of the fund, which denoted 'realty' and also had the personal touch of Tim, the founder of the fund. I was the first person to join the fund in India and I had to take care of the approvals, registrations, hunt for office space, recruitments and several other mundane activities all by myself. Tim had himself called me on the first day at my job; he was very warm and encouraging. I was charged up for my new role and assignment. God had been kind in giving me a second chance.

Within four months, the fund was up and running with an office on Golf Course Road in Gurgaon and a team of seven professionals. We hired a PR agency that did a good job of spreading awareness about us with the appropriate audience. We soon started receiving several requests every week for investments into various real estate projects across the country. Time and luck was with us. I have always believed that capability and values are of use only when the timing is right and luck is favourable. Real T seemed to have got all the elements in place.

While going through the investment requests one day, I came across a resort project in Goa. The location was excellent – right next to the ocean, with its own private beach. It had all the approvals in place, which was very impressive. I probed further to know more about the promoter and owner. It was mentioned in the last page of the proposal. Anu Grover.

I felt guilty for not having invited Anu for dinner as I had promised when I last met her. But life had taken such a turn soon after I had met her, and I was sure she would understand. I looked up her number in my contact list and called her up.

"Anu? This is Jeetu here!"

"Hey Jeetu! Good to hear from you. I have been missing all my dinners from the time we met in the hope that you might call anytime for our dinner meeting." Anu had a sharp memory and a sharper tongue.

"My apologies. Will explain when we meet. When is it convenient for you?"

"Tomorrow night sounds good. Taj on Man Singh Road at 8? I love the food at Varq."

"Done, see you tomorrow. Bye."

Later that night, I told Aashu about my dinner meeting with Anu. She did not react much to it, but just said softly, "You have just come out of a big trouble. Make sure you do not land in another."

I wore a tight fitting T-shirt and jeans for my dinner with Anu. I did not want it to be a very formal meeting, though I planned to discuss the Goa project. I reached Taj a few minutes before 8 p.m. and took the curved stairs down to Varq. Varq's ambience was a mix of modern day elegance and Mughal era opulence. I had heard the food was an even better fusion of the old and new.

Anu arrived a few minutes later. She was wearing a body hugging light brown chiffon *sari* with a matching sleeveless blouse. Her hair was shinier and longer than before, and she wore minimal make-up. Her sleeveless blouse allowed me to notice a small tattoo on her right upper arm. It was written, in small red letters, AG2. And there was a small heart at the end. I could immediately understand AG to be the initials of Anu Grover. But what could '2' mean, I wondered.

"Hey Anu, looking great as usual." I welcomed her as I pulled a chair for her.

"Thank you, and I can see your biceps have grown a bit bigger," she said smiling.

We both sat down. She ordered a glass of red Shiraz wine and I opted for my usual vodka and tonic water with Angostura bitters.

"I am really very sorry for the delay in calling you," I apologised again.

"No, I understand. You must have gotten busy," she said in an understanding tone.

"Actually I went through one of the worst phases of my life and my mind was totally occupied in that."

"Really? What happened, Jeetu?" Anu was genuinely concerned. She touched my hand gently.

I narrated the whole story to her as concisely as I could.

"Wow! This must have been terrible for you. Why didn't you call me during that time? Anu Grover is no less a tigress herself, you know." Her face had turned a little red. That moment my mind visualised the face of a tigress on her slender body.

"But it's over now, Anu. And I have joined as the Country Head of Real T in India," I informed Anu.

"Oh, have you? You didn't want to join my company? Probably too small for you! But I am happy for you. Especially after all that you had to go through."

"Anu, I wanted to talk to you about a proposal I received from your firm for the Goa project." I wanted to get down to business as soon as possible.

"Oh, yes. I remember we had sent it to Real T. Didn't know you were there. If I knew, I would have called you directly and asked you for the investment. Though you never invested your emotions in me, I am sure you would have invested your money in my project." She laughed loudly. I could see her twinkling eyes and bright white teeth.

"Let us order some food first. I would suggest that we go with the vegetarian appetisers and then fish curry and some crab meat. Is that fine with you, Jeetu?"

"I will go with your choice, Anu." I nodded.

"I wish I always got my choice." Anu sighed and then smiled a little while her tongue touched her red lips.

We talked about the Goa project for some time. When it comes to business, Anu becomes sharply focussed and her brain cells zoom in to the core issues and quickly separates the wheat from the chaff. Within half an hour, there was an in-principle agreement and the terms she had agreed on were scribbled on a napkin.

"There is your agreement, Mr Investor!" she said, handing me the napkin.

The food was lovely and definitely lived up to the reputation. There was a bowl of special yellow *dal* that was served complimentary, and Anu was more than happy to share from the same bowl. At the end of the main course, the waiter tempted us wickedly with a choice of desserts. I declined firmly but Anu ordered a piece of strawberry chocolate cake. The cake was larger compared to the portions of the main course dishes we had ordered. I could see Anu was enjoying her cake. I was cursing myself for not indulging in desserts that night. It must have been my tight T shirt, which prevented me from having any sinful dessert.

"Come on, have one spoon." She scooped out a large piece of cake in her spoon and brought it in front of my mouth as I was lost in my thoughts. It seemed she had read my mind.

I leaned over a bit and gladly had the full piece. She smiled and continued to finish the rest of her cake.

After she had finished the cake, we shook hands as a token of celebration and she raised a toast. "To many more deals and meals together!"

I was in a more relaxed mood after that. We decided to have our fourth drink.

"One for the road and the long journey ahead." She justified to me.

"You know Jeetu, in our youth, you fight with your body and aggression. But as you grow older, you fight with your mind and guile. You should remember that in your future fights,' said Anu and I could not agree more with her.

We were both a little high from our drinks by then. Anu was in no hurry to leave the restaurant.

"I know you must think that I am a cut-throat businesswoman. And a spoilt brat! But it's not like that all the time with all the people. I have deep feelings. Feelings so strong that I often have to disguise them under this image that I have. I have never had feelings for anybody else like I have for you Jeetu. I could have married anyone I wanted but I was and AM prepared to wait. Wait for my entire life, if need be," Anu said in one single breath.

I was taken aback by her persistent feelings for me after all these years. I had never seen her so soft, so vulnerable. I liked this side.

"Anu, you are one of the most desirable women I have ever met. Let me tell you that if there had been no Aashu, I would have been the happiest person to accept your love. But my bond with Aashu is simply unbreakable. We call it the TFT bond!"

"What? What the hell is a TFT bond?" She was slurring slightly.

"It's our bond based on trust, faithfulness and truth. We cannot break this bond, Anu. I am really sorry."

I asked the waiter to get the cheque and I made the payment quickly. I didn't want our discussions to continue further. I didn't want any more trouble in my life and Aashu's.

As we were leaving, I asked Anu when she had got her tattoo done.

"Hmm… just recently. Maybe around the time we last met." She was in her proper senses now.

"If you don't mind, what does the '2' in the tattoo mean?"

"So, you know what AG means?" She looked at me with a slight tilt on her head.

"Obviously Anu Grover!"

"Ha, you know me so little, dear. I will let you in on my little secret. I will kill you if you tell anyone. A is for Anu. And then it's G2. Or Jeetu," she said, pointing a finger towards me.

"You are mad! Anyway, it was a lovely dinner. And I look forward to closing our deal soon. You have a safe ride back home. Good night."

Her BMW car had reached the lobby porch to pick her up.

"Good night, dear," she said and gestured a flying kiss towards me.

I reached home. While having my late night customary glass of milk with Aashu, I told her about the dinner and the tattoo.

"She is mad," Aashu said in a low voice. She then kissed me on the left cheek and said, "I love you." Aashu had full faith in her hummingbird.

48

"Mr Mittal? This is David Anderson calling from Tim & Him. Is it a good time to talk?"

Tim & Him was a sister firm of Real T. It had the clear stamp of Tim on its name again. Tim & Him was purely into mergers and acquisitions (M&A) advisory services. I was told by a senior person at Real T in the US that Tim had started Tim & Him as a simple token of love for his lover. Tim was married many years ago and then got divorced. He had no children. A few months after his divorce, Tim came out of the closet and declared openly that he was gay. The 'Him' in Tim & Him apparently stood for Tim's lover who ran the firm and had an equal stake as Tim in the firm.

I was aware of Tim & Him's activities and sometimes would refer potential M&A opportunities involving India or Indians to the firm. Manoj Mittal was my reference. Most of these references were from my local investment banking friends in India who did not want to be named as a 'reference' to avoid any complication. However, if a deal was successful, I would take my friends out for a dinner. So far, I had taken only one of my investment banking friends out for a dinner over the last one year I had been at Real T.

"Hi David. Please just call me Manoj. Please tell me. How can I help you?" Manoj said politely but very slowly.

David had set up the meeting with Manoj at an Ethiopian restaurant in Manhattan. Over lunch, David explained to Manoj about a new start-up company in California that had discovered a unique formulation of a cream for rapid treatment of pimples. The company was started by a couple of very smart students from MIT just about a year ago. They had invested about hundred thousand dollars in the company which was now valued at two million dollars.

"20 times growth. And in one year? Impressive!" Manoj's interest was visible.

"And do you know who is backing them now? The wizard of private equity, Ramky himself! Ramky recently took 25 per cent stake in this company at the two million dollar valuation; he strongly believes that the company's valuation will go up at least 100 times more within a couple of years," David explained to Manoj.

Manoj's face lit up when he heard Ramky's name. Ramky had nearly a cult status among Indians residing in the US.

"So, how do I come into the picture?" Manoj asked David.

"Manoj, the original founders were interested in research only, and not in the day-to-day running and growing of the business. They want to just retain a 25 per cent stake for themselves and sell the balance 50 per cent they still hold for a million-dollar infusion into the company. And we thought this could be of interest to you."

"But why would Ramky not buy the balance 50 per cent himself? He can then find a CEO to run it."

"Ramky's style of investment is very simple and consistent. He strongly believes in the management having a skin in the game. He wants somebody capable running the business, like you, but also someone who puts in a significant financial commitment in the business. You would know Manoj, there is no substitute for hard cash. No stock options or shadow options have the same effect." David continued to explain.

Manoj was an MBA and understood the rationale. He had built a few successful businesses in India before migrating to the US and was looking for investment opportunities. This could be the perfect opportunity for him.

David showed Manoj a presentation of the facility, the team, and the financial statements of the previous year. He also gave Manoj all the supporting documents, which Manoj reviewed in detail later.

"I am keen on the deal. Can we visit California? And meet the team? And Ramky also?" Manoj called up David after a week.

The visit to California was arranged after 10 days. David accompanied Manoj to California. They drove to an office-cum-warehouse in the suburbs of San Jose from where the business was run. The two founders of the business greeted David and Manoj at the main gate with a lot of warmth. They even put garlands around

Manoj. The founders had many Indian friends at MIT and had obviously done their homework well on Indian traditions.

The founders introduced Manoj to the team and the finance manager who answered all the queries of Manoj. The finance manager handed over all the documents Manoj asked for. Manoj had a strong background in accounting and did not need any other accountant to do the due-diligence for him. But he wanted to see the efficacy of the product.

"Manoj, this is our test room. We are not allowed to go inside because of strict hygiene conditions, but you can watch from this glass window." One of the founders showed Manoj their testing area.

The test area had five people from diverse ethnic backgrounds with several pimples on their faces. The doctor inside the test area was wearing a mask and gloves. He put a white powder on the affected areas of the people in the test group. He left it like that for about half an hour. After half an hour, when the people washed their faces, there was a visible reduction in the size and redness of the pimples.

"This is amazing! In how much time will the pimple completely disappear?" Manoj asked the founders.

"In about two weeks' time, these people will be completely free from pimples for the rest of their lives!" One of the founders announced proudly.

"What if I want to test it on myself?" Manoj asked with a childish look.

"Oh, you will have to wait for a month or two then to get the required approvals from the authorities who are very strict on how and on whom the experiments are conducted."

"Of course. I was just joking." Manoj laughed.

"Come on, Manoj. Let me show you the vault area where we keep the special and secret formulation of this powder. Of course, when we start selling in the market, this powder will have to be converted into a cream form."

The vault area was in a secure far-end corner of a warehouse, with state-of-the-art electronic and physical security arrangements. The vault was opened briefly, and Manoj saw the white powder kept in large transparent plastic bags. Just then, Ramky made his entrance into the office.

"Manoj, it is indeed a pleasure to meet you. I have heard so many good things about you." Ramky shook hands vigorously with Manoj.

"The pleasure is entirely mine. I feel privileged." Manoj looked at Ramky with awe and admiration.

"Come, let's talk more over lunch?" Ramky suggested as it was nearing lunch time.

Lunch was served in the office cafeteria. It soon became obvious that Ramky and Manoj shared a strong positive vibe for each other. They were cracking jokes in Hindi and laughing, much to the embarrassment of David and the two founders.

"Manoj, if I can't share a joke with a person, I don't invest in him." Ramky shared his thoughts with Manoj.

"I absolutely understand. I am so proud that you find me capable to run this business." Manoj was indeed beaming with pride.

"I read your background that David had sent to me. It was very impressive. And once you committed to putting in million dollars in the business, I knew I had the right man. I did not need to do any more homework from my side. But you should make sure you do your homework properly, Manoj."

"If someone like you has invested in this business, I will be showing a torch to the sun by doing any more homework!" Both Manoj and Ramky laughed out loudly again.

Within a month, the whole deal was signed and sealed. Manoj shifted to San Jose. He rented out an apartment and took over the day-to-day running of the business from the founders. He was designated as the Managing Director and CEO. For the first couple of days, Manoj focussed on meeting the team members and just spending time with them. He also met the five people from the test and was very happy with their feedback. Manoj was very cautious and aware of the security of the vault where the powder was kept. He changed the locker code of the vault immediately, and decided to not share it with anybody.

On the third day, the receptionist at the office called and informed Manoj that there were two people from the government to see him. Manoj asked them to wait in the meeting room. He went to see them in a few minutes.

"Sir, we are from DEA. Drug Enforcement Administration. And we would like to check your vault for the powder you store there. Who has the locker code please?" One of the tall officers asked.

"Sure. I have the locker code. Let me escort you there," Manoj said confidently.

Manoj opened the vault locker and willingly showed the officers some samples of the powder. One of the officers sniffed and tasted the powder. He then turned around to Manoj and said, "Sir, you are under arrest for storing and distribution of illegal drugs."

49

"Thank you very much Tim. I really appreciate it from the core of my heart." I called up Tim early in the morning India time.

"You are most welcome, Jeetu. I perhaps have more sentiments and feelings than people would like to give me credit for," Tim said, as he ran on the treadmill. He continued, "You take care of yourself Jeetu and our business in India, of course. The justice system in the US will now take care of Atul Katiyal."

Justice was served. A little late and may be at a different place. But it was served. We had to now wait for the punishment to be served. Atul Katiyal may have thought that his new identity as Manoj Mittal would save him, but I had a promise to keep.

"Aashu, wake up! I have some great news for you. Atul Katiyal has been arrested in the US finally. I have kept my promise to you."

Aashu was wide awake by now. She was aware of my plans and activities over the past year in trying to track down and trap Atul.

Aashu was delirious and started dancing on the bed. We were both kind, generous and forgiving people at heart. But Atul was no ordinary thief. He had robbed us not only of our hard-earned money but also of our faith and trust in humanity. It would take a long time for both the wealth and faith to return. We could not show mercy to such a person. Mercy is only shown to those who realise they have made a mistake and are repentant about it. Atul had no such regrets. For him, this was only a stepping stone for his other plans and ambitions. We were stepped and trampled upon but he could not crush our souls, our spirit.

Our landline phone rang. It was Ramky.

"Jeetu! I have never felt so happy in closing a deal, that too where I lose money," Ramky exclaimed.

"I know I don't need to say thanks to you Ramky but you did go out of your way this time. God bless you." I was choked with emotions.

It had been an emotional ride for the past year. I had made a promise to Aashu to punish Atul Katiyal but I had no idea where he was. I had to keep my calm and be prepared for the long haul. I hired Atul's ex brother-in-law into Real T as an accounts executive as soon as I joined the firm. He then went out of his way to trace the whereabouts of Atul. He was able to let me know within a couple of months that Atul had fled to the US under a new name Manoj Mittal.

For the next couple of months, I had no idea how to find Manoj Mittal in the US. Then, as luck or *karma* would have it, I came to know that Neha *didi's* son had gone to the US for his higher studies and then had married an American girl working in the Department of Homeland Security. I was not sure of contacting him given the slight bitterness Neha *didi* had with our family after her miserable marriage that had been forced by *baba*. But *didi's* son was more than helpful; he even remembered attending our wedding. He was able to convince his wife to help me. She was able to provide me the address and other coordinates of Atul Katiyal in New York.

I hired a private investigator in New York to provide me with information about Atul Katiyal before I laid out my trap for him. The investigator did a great job and found that Atul had taken treatment from a reputed neurologist for his palilalia induced speech disorder. He had improved miraculously; he just had to speak slowly. He had lost a lot of weight during the treatment. His pimples had reduced too but they still bothered him. He had circulated his CV to many firms for employment but his tourist visa status was a problem. Atul's CV was embellished with his corporate turnarounds and start-up success stories in India. He soon realised that the best way for him to secure a long-term legal stay in the US was to invest in some local business.

This was enough background for me to hatch a plan together with Ramky, with a little help from Tim. Ramky spent a lot of time, effort and money in renting an office, doing all the paperwork and documentation, hiring a team of actors, providing funds through another financial institution for the initial 100,000 dollars equity, and taking care of several other smaller details. He knew that almost the entire one million dollars he was putting into the company and other related expenditure would never be recovered. But I was sure the pleasure of Atul losing million dollars and facing a long jail term would more than make up for the loss of money for Ramky.

Atul Katiyal's case was put on fast track and the conviction was announced within three months of his arrest. He was found guilty on the charges of drug trafficking, forgery and cheating the US Immigration. He was given a prison sentence of 18 years.

Aashu looked at me when she heard this news from Ramky and said, "I love you so much Jeetendra Singh… so much Jeetendra Singh."

We asked Ramky for one last favour on this issue. I explained to him over email what we wanted to do. And then Aashu personally spoke to Ramky on the phone.

"Hi Ramky. Can you please have that bought and sent to Atul Katiyal in prison? I know it won't be easy to do so and he may not be allowed to take it with him inside the prison, but at least let Atul know what he received from us as the last gift." Aashu requested Ramky. And I knew Ramky would somehow manage to get it done.

A week later, Atul Katiyal's name was called out in the prison. He came to the counter to receive the gifts and a note sent from us.

'Dear Atul. I know you must be missing my mutton *biryani*. So sending you a special mutton *biryani* made only from goat testicles. Maybe this help you be reborn as a proper man in the next life. Aashu.'

The note was written on a card placed on top of the packaged *biryani*.

'Dear Atul. I had once made a promise to you, if you remember, to help you get into a new business. I fulfilled that promise. I am also sending you a special pimple reduction cream which you may need more in prison to keep yourself beautiful for your manly inmates. Jeetu.'

The note was written on a white piece of paper which was wrapped around a pimple cream tube.

50

I was really enjoying my work at Real T. It had been almost two years with Real T and my team had managed to invest successfully in more than 20 projects. We had also invested in Anu Grover's Goa project and we were ready to exit from it with a handsome return. Anu and I sometimes talked over phone about business and the Goa project, but we did not meet after that dinner at Varq.

I came to know about Anu's new and lavish high-end resort on the outskirts of Gurgaon, at the base of the Aravalli ranges. I was glad Anu was doing well in her business. She may not have been successful in love but her grit and determination had certainly brought her success in business. Anu had also started a foundation for social work in the area of women's empowerment, and most of her earnings went towards the cause of this foundation. Anu may not marry again, she may not have children of her own, but she was definitely leaving a strong legacy behind her.

Aashu and I were proud of our legacy too. Aarvee was a teenager now and had become very tall. In fact, he had become taller than me too. A father always feels great pride when his child becomes taller than him. A mother always feels proud when her child starts looking like her. Aarvee had a combination of good genes from Aashu and me. He had a good personality coupled with Aashu's good looks and skin. And most importantly, Aarvee had the inner strength and values that both Aashu and I so deeply valued. It was early days for Aarvee but the die was cast well.

I always tell my colleagues at work this. In business, everyone keeps complaining of not having enough resources. Either money is in short supply or material or talent. Nature never complains. It just goes about its task like an efficient manager and maximises the output from the given resources and constraints. Nature had definitely done a good job with Aarvee.

Aashu was now ready to go back to work again. She had interviewed for the post of Chief Marketing Officer at a new ecommerce start-up in Gurgaon and was recently made an attractive offer. She had to go to office only three days a week. The other two days she could work from home. And she had the weekend to herself. It was a big change from her earlier stint of working six days a week.

"Life is taking a new turn, Jeetu. I am both happy and scared to go back to work," Aashu confessed.

"Why should YOU be scared? If anyone, it is your competitors who should be scared."

"You are always so encouraging. I wonder what I would have done without you in my life," she said, half in jest.

"You would have simply waited for me till I came into your life. But tell me Aashu, what would have happened if you had got married to someone else and then met me?" I liked to ask such hypothetical questions to Aashu.

"I would have got you married to Anu Grover. Happy?"

"You could have done that, my dear. But before that, I would have either killed your husband or killed myself."

"Oh oh! So brave! See, I saved you then from going to prison." Aashu continued, "Though living in an unhappy marriage is also like living in prison. Or even worse."

"Yes, I completely agree. Look at Jasraj and Rakhi now. Both were so happy when they got married. But for the past few months, they have both been miserable. They look less healthy, they socialise much less, and get angry much more. I have never seen Jasraj so irritable and sad."

It was difficult to have a proper conversation with Jasraj lately. His attention span had reduced a lot and his grouchiness was much talked about in office.

"Yes, I heard about them. It's so sad. I guess all these very rich and successful people like Anu or Jasraj, they find it difficult to compromise. And without compromise there can be no successful marriage," Aashu said.

"Well, it's not with these rich and successful people alone. What happened to Neha *didi* or closer home to *chachu* and *choti chachi*?" I countered.

"What's meant to happen will happen. Birth, marriage, and death are the only three milestones God sets clearly. Whatever happens in between these three milestones is a matter of chance and permutation-combination." Aashu had become a lot more philosophical lately.

"Well, why are we both getting so sad and sombre? Before I start my new job, let us spend the weekend at that new resort near the Aravallis?" Aashu was referring to Anu Grover's resort.

"That's a great idea. Aarvee can stay here with his grandparents, so we can have more fun there."

I pinched Aashu on her waist.

My parents had come home for a few days. They were always happy to spend time with Aarvee on their own. My mother was getting a little weak due to old age; it pained me to see her walk slowly, with a slight limp. But that did not stop her from making sure she poured oil on my hair oil every Tuesday morning and massaged it gently. Her head massage always stirred memories of the past, of Jamshedpur, of school days.

My father had taken to commentary. Commentary on the state of political affairs in this country and how Indian cricketers could play better. He read at least three newspapers every day. Aarvee tried to get him hooked to online news but he said, "The pleasure of touch and feel is far higher than just visual medium." I assumed he meant the newspaper and there was indeed no hidden pun in his words.

Late Saturday morning we drove to this new resort. I had picked up this habit from Anu who would sometimes make her driver sit in the rear seat while she drove herself. It is more comfortable to be in the driver's seat. You feel in control. Anu Grover always liked to be in control.

The resort was like an oasis in the desert with cottages atop a tree or on a small pond. Each cottage was unique. There was a 50-acre forest area within the resort with some lovely walking trails. We chose a cottage just by the side of the forest, overlooking a large oval shaped swimming pool. The fresh air, the bright sunlight, the light cool breeze, the smell of manure and organic crops grown nearby, and the constant chirping of the birds were a source of immediate relaxation to both of us. We had seen many ups and downs in life in the past few years and we deserved such heavenly pampering.

We decided to have lunch first before checking into our cottage. The lunch was a spectacular buffet of Indian and Chinese food. Most of the vegetables were from the organic farm in the resort. After all these years, I finally gave up my middle-class mindset of overeating at buffets. I focussed only on the salads, while Aashu had some soup and vegetables. It is not only one's mindset, I thought. It is also the body that changes with time and feels better and lighter with less food. After a simple and tasty lunch, we walked towards the cottage.

Our cottage had a big bed, with crisp, clean, white bed sheets. The furniture was simple yet elegant and largely made of teak wood, other than the cushy leather sofa in one corner of the room facing the TV. The sofa immediately rekindled memories of our honeymoon. I sat down on the sofa. Aashu came and sat on my thighs facing me, with her hands resting on my shoulders.

"I am going to break our rule today, Jeetu. Thank you," Aashu bent forward and whispered into my ears.

"Thank you for what?"

"For everything. For our marriage. For Aarvee. For this life."

We then kissed each other, slowly and passionately. She seemed in a different mood that day.

"Darling, let me just come back from the bathroom. And then we can put up the 'Do Not Disturb' sign on our door till dinner time." It was just 3 in the afternoon.

I took a quick bath, brushed my teeth, wore my *kurta pyjama*, and rushed back to the bed. Aashu was busy reading something on her phone; she had a slight look of worry on her face.

"What's wrong, Aashu?"

"Oh nothing, just deleting some old messages." I could see her press the delete button. "That was the last one."

"Good, now let us not get distracted," I said in a seemingly stern voice.

"Jeetu, don't be mad now. But can I take a half hour walk in the woods? I am feeling very suffocated here and need some fresh air. I promise I shall be back soon," she said and kissed my forehead.

"Okay, but come back soon. Or I will be asleep and you can come in my dreams only."

She wore her walking shoes and put on her sunglasses, and then looked at me from the door as she walked out.

"Make sure no one enters your heart while I am away Jeetu." She stood at the door and said.

"I promise, dear! As long your protection coating is there, no one can enter my heart." I replied with a smile.

"I will always be there to protect you," she said, blowing a flying kiss, and then she closed the door.

51

Someone was banging loudly at the door of our cottage. I got up startled from the small nap I had taken while Aashu was away on her walk.

"Who is it?" I shouted from my bed.

"Sir, I am the resort manager, and you need to come with me immediately."

I opened the door and found the manager panting and sweating in the afternoon sun.

"Sir, please come with me straightaway. There is some problem with your wife."

"What's the matter? Where are we going? What's happened to Aashu, my wife?" I was nearly shouting at the manager as we ran towards the back entrance of the resort.

I could see a few other staff of the resort assembled in a circle just outside the back entrance gate. The back entrance was usually unmanned as there was just a vast barren area outside. Somebody at the resort had told me earlier that the owner of the resort was keen to buy out the barren area and expand the resort.

The resort manager pushed the other staff and held my hands as he pointed to the ground below. Aashu was lying there in a pool of blood with a bullet pierced through the front of her forehead. This could not be real. This must be one of my dreams. God cannot be so cruel to take my Aashu away from me so early. I was feeling dizzy by now and fainted soon after.

I regained consciousness within a few minutes. I saw somebody sprinkling water on me from a bottle. I immediately took the bottle from his hand and sat down. I lifted Aashu's head and put it on my lap. I poured water on her lips and started to cry loudly, "Aashu, I have brought water for you. Sip it. Sip it with your lips. But do not embark on this journey without me." My memory flashed back to the past and I remembered her words about me giving her water before her final journey.

I tore my *kurta* and tried to cover the bullet wound on her forehead with it. I tried to shake her, reminded her of Aarvee, kissed her, and reminded her of the promises she had made to me but she was motionless. I looked up at the sky and started to curse, "You have no system of fairness and justice. *Karma* is a soulless and heartless computer program, nothing more than that! And a faulty computer program! You should have fixed the bug in your program before you sent *karma* looking for my innocent Aashu. I hate you! I hate you!" And then I looked down at Aashu, and cried aloud, "I love you Aashu, and always will." I fainted again only to recover after an hour in a hospital in Gurgaon.

"Sir, I am afraid your wife was brought here dead. We have informed the police and they are here for the investigations," a senior doctor at the hospital informed me.

My parents and Aarvee were sitting beside me in the hospital room where I was kept. My mother was sobbing and Aarvee was sitting next to her and holding my mother's hand tight. My father was standing with the doctor. As soon as the doctor left, my father came closer to me and whispered, "You have to be strong for Aarvee."

I gestured to Aarvee to come near me. Aarvee was a strong boy and had controlled his emotions well so far. He sat on my bed, and said, "*Papa*, please tell her I will not eat any more junk food and I will do very well in my studies." And he started crying aloud. I wanted him to cry. I held him closely with both my arms and consoled him, "Aarvee, your mother is just on another side journey. We will meet her again at the main station soon for another journey together."

I wanted to cry again with Aarvee but I had to hold back my tears inside. I had often cried in movies but there was always a subconscious relief in my mind that it was not real. But that day I had no such relief. That was real. There was no dam to hold my tears. It had burst with all its fury. Aashu had been the balm for all my pains. She would either put ointment on the pain area, give me something herbal to eat or drink, massage my head gently, or just smile and share a joke. But that day I had no such balm. My life was going to be in pain for a long time.

Aashu had pledged her eyes and heart after her death. I often told her that the two most beautiful parts in her body were her eyes and her heart. On my 40th birthday, she gifted me the organ donation pledge. She then said, "My eyes and my heart will always be around you when I die." I did not want this gift now. I wanted her in whole and not her body parts within shells of other souls. My father comforted me, "Son, you have to respect her wishes." I was in no condition to argue with my father or anyone. I only wanted to argue with God. Is this how he wants to keep reminding us of his presence? Did he do this because I doubted the dreams he had planted in my head? In a weird way, I was feeling satisfied that Aashu was contributing to science even after death. I wanted this science to prove to me that there was no God.

Dadu and Aashu's mother could not stop crying during the cremation. My mother asked me to console them. Aarvee stared at the smoke arising from the pyre. He was, like me perhaps, trying to catch a last glimpse of Aashu. During the cremation, I realised that Jasraj had not called me or even come for the cremation. I needed my friend the most at this time.

The next day, I asked my assistant at office to inform Jasraj again. She called me back shortly with another shocking news, "Sir, Mr Jasraj has met with some accident it seems. He has lost all temporary memory. He was actually found walking alone near one of the malls in Gurgaon a couple of days ago."

I was sure now that there was no God. I did not need science to prove it to me. My wife, my soul mate was physically dead. And my close friend, my man support, was mentally disturbed.

I wandered around my home at night hoping to catch some glimpse of Aashu while she still hovered around in this planet. But all I could catch were more memories of the past. Memories that seemed so normal, so boring, so routine. Memories of her bringing my polished shoes when I was in a hurry to go to work, memories of her feeding me while I was on a business conference call on my phone. Memories of her sitting by Aarvee's bed all through the night when he had a stomach infection, memories of her giving me half the bread and omelette from her breakfast served on the flight so that I could have a more fulsome breakfast. Memories of her pressing my clothes with one hand while calling the grocery delivery person with her other hand. Memories of her bringing my late night glass of milk every day without fail, memories of her fasting for two days at a stretch every year so that I could live long. If only God had given me a chance, I would have fasted for a whole month for Aashu. If only she could be with me now…

I was a complete wreck for almost a week. I then remembered another of Baba's wise statements. "Do you know why I still remain so happy after your grandmother died so early? So that she can be happy up there knowing I am happy."

I knew Aashu would never be happy seeing me like the wreck I was. Aarvee had adjusted and accepted much better than I had. He had his whole life ahead of him, he will fill these memories with happier ones in the times to come. What will I fill my memory with? At that instant, I decided that for Aashu's sake, for Aarvee's sake, for my parents' sake, I needed to be strong and get my life back in order. I knew the answer for future. I will refill my memories of Aashu. And not let anyone else enter my heart. This was going to be my last gift to her. Keeping my last promise to her that I would not let anyone enter my heart. I knew though that she could not keep her last promise to me while alive.

I was happy in a way that Anu Grover did not call me up after Aashu's demise. I was weak and vulnerable, and did not want Anu to take advantage of that in any way. Had I not made the last promise to Aashu, I could have thought of exploring a future with Anu. But now I was bound by a promise. However, Anu had no such constraints. I was surprised that she was not making any move from her side. Especially knowing that her resort had a part in all this. Maybe she had found someone else as a companion. Whatever it was, I was happy she away from me.

I was not at all happy with the investigations done by the crime police department of Gurgaon. Sub-inspector Vinay Singh was the investigating officer. He could find no clue or motive for the murder. He had interviewed all the staff at the resort, as well as checked the closed circuit TV cameras that captured the images of all guests entering from the main gate. There was no camera at the back entrance. He found no other trace or witness near the site of the crime. He was going to file a report of accidental shooting from some hunter in the barren area where people sometimes shot birds. Or it could have been a simple case of a failed robbery. He was to put both the possibilities in his report. I was very angry at this and knew this meant the investigation would be closed. I met Vinay Singh at the police station.

"Vinay *ji*, I don't think you have conducted your investigations properly. This is a clear case of murder. You should take more time and then file your report," I told him angrily.

"Sir *ji*, we know our job. We know whom to suspect and whom not to. You could have been our main suspect. But we did not trouble you, did we?" Vinay did not look up at me while reading his newspaper.

"I am ready for any investigations. I am not afraid!"

"Sir *ji*, once you get two slaps from me, then all your fear will come rushing out. I would have liked nothing more than slapping you, dragging you on to the main road, and putting you inside lock-up under my custody for a week at least. I would have made sure that you wrote what I told you and be charged for the murder of your wife. Then the case would drag on for years while you rotted in jail. I did not do all this only because the resort owner wanted to me close the case soon as it was affecting her business. And she also made me promise that I would not bother you. You filthy animal born to the wildest animals of the jungle!" Vinay was red with anger. I was shocked by his reaction.

I just stood there speechless, and then asked him, "Who are you Vinay Singh?"

"I am the nephew of Ram Singh. My uncle was a driver with your *baba* and was murdered in cold blood by him," he replied.

Karma was not ready to let go of us so easily.

52

I tried putting pressure on Vinay Singh through some senior IPS officers I knew from my business networks. But a man driven by revenge is hungrier and more ruthless than a man driven by the need for justice. Vinay Singh tactfully managed to placate his seniors and stuck to the same line of investigation. He had no other motivation than to close this case. He could not put me behind bars like he wanted to but he at least managed to make me feel helpless.

I hired a private investigator but he was not able to make any progress. He had no particular suspect to start with. I tried to recount our enemies from the past who could be potential suspects. Atul Katiyal could not possibly manage such a crime sitting from a secured US prison. Bhola was certain about not ever hearing from Tiger Mahajan. *Chachu* would never do such a thing. I could not think of any enemy for Aashu also. We were back to where we had started from. Could Vinay Singh's theory and hypothesis be true? But what if it's not true? Would Aashu ever forgive me for not finding her killer?

I has started going to work, while my parents managed the house and took care of Aarvee also. I would come back late from work, and then have my vodka and tonic water. I no longer needed the bitters – I was full of bitterness myself. I tried to put on a happy face in front of my parents and Aarvee, but they knew I was burning from inside. Nothing could douse that fire. That fire of uncertainty and justice not been done. I did my exercises at home. I taught Aarvee a few exercises.

My mind exercised round-the-clock thinking of what could have had happened that fateful day. I began to lose weight rapidly. About 20 per cent of the body's energy is consumed by the brain. And my brain just could not stop consuming the energy from the rest of my body.

Most nights I could not sleep, and the nights in which I did manage to sleep, I would keep praying for some dream, some hint of what had happened. I knew I would never have a dream from the past.

The lack of sleep, the constant stress, and the long hours at work started to take a toll on my health. I went for a complete health-check up on my father's insistence, and the doctors found my condition to be alarming due to the stress levels. My thyroid level was high and the cholesterol was well over the normal range. The doctors put me on immediate medication and a regime of healthy lifestyle.

I could have all the medicines in the world and I could follow all the advice for a healthy life, but all of it has no use if the inner soul is not ready to fight. My inner soul was missing Aashu. My soul was missing its soulmate.

After a week, I got up feeling very fresh one morning. And I remembered a dream again after a very long time. I saw myself sitting in front of the desktop computer at home, thinking about my theory of Point Ten Zeros Six Nine. I could not make much sense of the dream. But I was confident that this was a sign, a premonition. No more doubts, no more scientific and rational analysis. I may be having my ongoing fight with God but I was now a complete believer in my premonitions. My health was under threat of further deterioration, and my premonition had come in a timely manner to help me fight this threat.

I went and sat in front of my home computer for a long time. Maybe I was supposed to open some file or email related to Aashu. I had already checked all of Aashu's emails in the hope of finding any lead of a suspect. But there was nothing in there. I didn't remember her using the computer much other than to browse the internet or log on to her Facebook page sometimes. As I sat there for some time, my eyes wandered to Aarvee's painting of Aashu on the wall. Aarvee was a gifted artist and he had made a beautiful black and white portrait of his mother.

I often saw Aarvee sitting in front of the portrait and thinking. I remembered Aashu's interest in painting and how she had taken up some professional painting lessons. She had lost interest in it soon, but I remembered her talking about scanning and saving a painting in a password protected file in the computer.

I started searching for this file. I soon saw a file named 'mydreampaintings'. The word 'dream' in the file somehow resonated strongly with my sixth sense and my own dream. I clicked on it to open the file. It asked for the password. I tried all combinations of Aashu's name and my name and Aarvee's name, with the addition of the '@' sign, numbers in our dates of birth or a simple '123'. Nothing worked. I then typed 'Point Ten Zeros Six Nine'. It did not work. I tried 'Point000000000069'. This also did not work. I then tried 'Point10zeros69'. It worked and opened. I should have thought of this before. Aashu always had the habit of starting a password with a word and then adding a number behind. She found balance in this. The balance of words and numbers. Of the left and right brains.

The file opened. There was only one scanned copy of a painting as I had expected. It was the painting of a security guard praying to Shiva's *lingam* in an open area adjoining the forest. I could not figure out much from this painting. Maybe the dream was just about opening this painting, remembering Aashu, and feeling good. It did feel good. But I was not sure how long this feeling would last.

I went about my daily chores and came back home late at night. I had dinner but I did not need my vodka that day. I talked to Aarvee about his school and his basketball training. Aarvee was a good basketball player and he was a captain of the Junior North Zone basketball team.

"*Papa*, I am okay with all the subjects at school, except Hindi. I don't know why I need to learn Hindi." Aarvee complained.

"Hindi is our national language and it is a very beautiful language. It will help you in future," I tried to explain.

"Did you know that Lord Shiva has 1008 names in Hindi? I don't know how knowing these names will help me in the future." Aarvee had inherited Aashu's logical thinking.

"Okay, okay. Have your dinner first and then go to bed early. And I promise not to sing you a Hindi lullaby!" I patted his back, and Aarvee kissed me on the forehead. "I love you, *papa*. Good night."

I went to bed with a slightly relaxed mind that night. I slept for almost six hours without any disturbance. As I woke up, my subconscious mind had worked through the night and it provided me with a summary insight. Bhola is another name of Shiva and Bhola knows a security guard. There was only one security guard whom Bhola had recommended to me once when I had gone to Jamshedpur.

I called up Bhola immediately.

"Bhola, how are you?"

"Sir, I am fine. But I am very upset and angry to hear about the incident. Sir, you just find out who did this or who you think could have done this and I will have fast-track justice done."

"It's fine, Bhola. Don't worry about that now. I just want to know about the security guard you had once recommended to me? Where is he?"

"Oh, you mean Manoj Pandey, sir? Son of Raghuvar Pandey? Thank you, sir. He had joined your company and he is still there."

"Bhola, I want you to come to Delhi by the next train. Can you do it?"

"Sir, you only have to order."

Bhola arrived in two days. By then, I had found out more about Manoj Pandey from the Synfra leadership team for security services. Manoj was a security supervisor who sometimes worked as a personal security officer of important people since he possessed a pistol licence. Manoj was part of the team that was deputed for Anu Grover's business. He often worked as a PSO for Anu herself. He was very loyal to Anu, I heard.

Bhola called Manoj Pandey on his mobile and asked him to come to a hotel on Sohna Road on Sunday morning. Bhola and I received Manoj at the hotel gate itself. We asked him to sit in the rear seat of my SUV. He looked a bit nervous at first but Bhola told him to calm down and not worry. I drove him towards Anu Grover's resort. Bhola kept Manoj engaged in stories of Jamshedpur. My mind was too occupied with anticipation and I did not hear a word of what Bhola told him. Once we reached the resort, we parked the car in the front and walked along the perimeter of the resort's fence and reached the back entrance area.

Manoj became very restless when he reached the spot where I had found my Aashu dead. He started to sweat although it was a reasonably cool day. He suddenly fell at my feet and started crying, "Sir, I have not done anything. Please believe me. Please save me."

53

Bhola asked Manoj to get up and face him.

"Manoj, I got you a job because of your father Raghuvar Pandey. He was a man of such strong values. I had saved his life once as you know. You now have to save Jeetu sir's life. His life has no meaning till he knows the truth. I will not beat you up to get the truth. I just want you to remember your father and then tell me the truth." Bhola was very calm and peaceful as he said this. But I knew he would take no time to beat up Manoj if he did not come out with the truth soon.

"Bhola *ji*, I am bound by a promise to someone who pays for my food. How can I break that promise?' Manoj told Bhola.

"Okay, you don't break your promise. But I will break every bone you have," Bhola said. And he slapped Manoj so hard that Manoj fell on the ground.

"This time we will not let you get up till you promise to tell us the truth," Bhola shouted and started kicking Manoj in the stomach.

I had a *déjà vu* feeling. I was reminded of the time when Bhola and I had beaten up that boyfriend of

Nirupama's. It was a fight for honour and ego then; it was a fight for truth and justice for Aashu now. I could go to any extent in this fight. I took out my belt and started hitting Manoj with it, with all my strength.

"Sir, Bhola *ji*, please spare me. I promise to tell you the truth." Manoj pleaded with folded hands while we continued to rain blows.

"Get up Manoj, and this time just the truth for the peace of your dead father's soul," Bhola roared at him.

"Sir, I came to this area often because Anu ma'am wanted me to negotiate with some of the farmers owning this barren land. Sometimes I would have my lunch here and take some rest. I loved the trees bordering the boundary fence from the outside. That day too, I was here resting just behind the tree over there." Manoj pointed to a tree on the boundary fence of the resort.

As Bhola and I were interrogating Manoj, Anu Grover was driving her car on the road leading from the Gurgaon-Faridabad road towards Surajkund. She had not been her usual self for the past few weeks, people close to her said. She was driving very fast, as if trying to escape from something.

"And what did you see Manoj that day?" I asked sternly.

"Sir, I saw a lady walking from inside the resort towards this entrance. And then I saw a man waiting outside the boundary fence. The lady met this man and asked him angrily how he could send her such a message. She asked him how he could write that he would commit suicide or kill somebody if she did not meet him. I also remember her saying that she would protect her husband from mad men like him, and that is why she had come there alone, without telling her husband about the message." Manoj recollected everything clearly. Bhola stood by his side.

I then remembered Aashu deleting an SMS message before she had stepped out. So this was the message. But Aashu could have shared it with me. She wanted to protect me but she had broken a key foundation of our cardinal TFT rule – to be truthful to each other. *Karma* has a fixed formula. It does not understand the context or the motive. Maybe Aashu could have been saved had she not broken our TFT bond. But I knew she would break the bond only if she feared for my life; she would not have cared for her life in any case.

Anu continued to increase her speed. Her driver seating in the rear seat was worried and kept requesting her to slow down. But nobody ever told Anu how fast to go. She continued pressing the accelerator.

"Sir, she also said that she was totally faithful to her husband. And that he should forget her forever."

"And then what happened?" Bhola shook him by the neck.

"Sir, the man became sad but he said he would try and forget her because he loved her so much. And at that time, Anu ma'am suddenly came near the tree from behind, around the bend of the boundary fence, from where she could hear what the lady and the man were talking. Anu ma'am used to sometimes come alone to inspect this barren land. The man continued talking to the lady and said that he loved her madly and would do whatever she said."

Anu's car swerved sharply round a corner, and a group of monkeys shrieked and jumped on either side of the road. The monkeys were used to getting fruits thrown from the cars passing by the corner. They were not used to a mad woman driving this fast as if to escape from the destiny following her.

"The man then tried to hug the lady. This is when Anu ma'am clicked a photograph of them together and said she was going to tell everything to you, Jeetu sir. The man got very angry and pulled out a pistol from under his shirt. That is when I stepped out and stood in front of Anu ma'am. But this man began to abuse Anu ma'am very badly sir," Manoj vividly described the chain of events.

"Then something happened, sir. Anu ma'am pulled the pistol hanging from the holster around my waist and took aim at this man."

There was another Range Rover coming from the opposite direction. Anu's car was about a kilometre away from the Range Rover. The vehicle was coming at a rapid speed, with the driver and a passenger sitting in the front seats. Anu did not slow down.

"Go on!" I shouted at Manoj.

"Sir, Anu ma'am's aim was not correct and the bullet went and hit the lady's forehead." Manoj looked down as he said this.

"The lady was obviously my wife, Aashu. Who was this man? Do you know him?" I asked.

A dog crossed the road in front of the Range Rover and the driver pressed hard on his brakes. The car turned 90 degrees and came straight in line of Anu's car, which was coming at a breakneck speed. Anu knew she could not stop now. She had to hit the Range Rover. She saw the passenger in the Range Rover; he too saw Anu in that fleeting moment.

"Do you know this man, Manoj?" I shouted again at Manoj.

"Yes sir. I think it was Jasraj sir."

Anu recognised Jasraj in the Range Rover which his driver was driving. Jasraj too saw Anu and probably recognised her in the momentary state of shock. His driver recalled later that Jasraj's last words were, "Forgive me God. Forgive me Aashu. Forgive me Jeetu."

Anu and Jasraj were both killed in that accident.

54

Ramky could not come for Aashu's cremation but he flew down as soon as he found the time. We had spoken for long hours on the phone and he was very supportive as usual. But I wanted to meet him, hug him, and cry my heart out. So, when he came out of the airport, I greeted him, hugged him, and cried for at least five minutes. Ramky was not a very emotional person but that day he could not stop himself from crying.

On the drive to my house, Ramky was silent for most of the time till he saw an accident of two small cars on the highway, which had brought traffic to a standstill.

"Maybe you are right, Jeetu. *Karma* does work in its own strange ways."

We both looked at each other and I understood what he meant. We both nodded our heads.

"Have I ever told you Ramky about that incident when Anu Grover and I had gone to a site visit and she was about to fall down before I saved her? She dramatically said, "You have saved my life and may my life be taken if I ever hurt you." Or something like that."

"That's why it is said that one should think before speaking. You never know how and when your words may come back to haunt you." Ramky was still in a pensive mood.

We reached the house and my mother opened the door. Ramky touched her feet while she blessed him from her heart. My mother knew everything about Ramky from me.

We sat down in the living room while my mother went to make some tea for us.

"Jeetu, I know at this time you would be thinking that you are as one of the unluckiest persons alive. But think of it positively. You have a great career. A great son. You have never hurt anyone intentionally. You have a good professional reputation. You are gifted with certain abilities such as premonitions."

"And I have a great friend like you Ramky." I tried to make us both smile.

"Yes, you indeed do!" Ramky smiled for the first time.

"But Ramky, all of these still do not fill the gap left by Aashu."

"I understand. But how many people have been lucky enough to spend so many years with someone they love so deeply? Not me for sure! And you now know the truth behind Aashu's death, and God has served the swiftest justice on those who were involved in it. How many people in India have this privilege? It takes decades and decades for justice to be done here."

Ramky was right. I should end my fight with God, I thought. I excused myself from Ramky. I took out a photograph of Aashu and kept it on the side of the small shrine in our house. Aashu used to spend at least half an hour every day praying in front of the shrine. I folded my hands in prayer and made a request to God. "Please do take care of my Aashu till we meet in the next life time."

After lunch, we decided to meet Rakhi at the Vasant Kunj farmhouse where she was still staying. Rakhi welcomed us warmly and guided us to the terrace on the first floor. The terrace was shaded by a large overhanging banyan tree. We sat down and had some freshly cut fruits brought by one of the many attendants in the farmhouse.

"Rakhi, I am extremely sorry for your loss," I looked at Rakhi and said.

"Thank you. I am very sorry too for Aashu," Rakhi replied.

"Jeetu, you are a good man. I don't want to hide anything from you," Rakhi continued. "Jasraj and I began fighting regularly after the dinner at your place. I could see clearly that Jasraj was infatuated by Aashu. In one of our fights, he angrily admitted that Aashu was the only real love in his life; he had had a crush on her from the school days in JDS in Kolkata. Aashu was a year senior to Jasraj at school and she probably never even knew about him."

My mind raced back to the various conversations between Jasraj and myself. The high school crush that he had, the various veiled compliments about Aashu, his desire to pray for a wife like Aashu in future, and many more such memories swept my mind.

"Had it not been for your Jeetu, Jasraj would have stopped at nothing to get Aashu. You knew him well."

I knew Jasraj well but clearly not well enough. I could, however, now understand why Jasraj had once said that I would make a great pair with Anu or how he was happy to offer a job to Aashu later.

"His fights with me increased after his frustration with his investments in movies and involvement in politics. In politics, however successful or rich you are, you are after all a servant of the High Command or a servant of the billions of people. Jasraj could not be either. Then, on the day he went to meet Aashu, he had a very nasty fight with me which almost became physical. He then said that he did not want to become an animal. He said he had no choice but to convince Aashu somehow."

Rakhi had a tinge of sadness on her face.

Rakhi then got up, went inside her room, and brought Jasraj's mobile phone. She opened the last message that Jasraj had written to Aashu.

'Dear Aashu *ji*. I have to admit. I have been your greatest lover since the JDS days when I was a year junior to you. I am going to divorce Rakhi shortly and I want to live with you only forever. If you refuse, then I will either commit suicide or just kill somebody. I am waiting outside the back entrance of your resort. Jasraj.'

Aashu had received this message just a few days after my light-hearted conversation with her. I had joked that if she had married someone else, I would have either committed suicide or killed her husband. I could understand why Aashu may have become so concerned after this SMS message. It was not for her own self, but for my protection. I shed a tear as I remembered her last words to me, "I will always be there to protect you."

Ramky did not speak a word throughout the entire conversation. We decided to leave soon and not make it more uncomfortable for Rakhi. Before leaving, I just asked her, "Rakhi, do you have a nephew studying in Gurgaon?"

Rakhi had a surprised look on her face. "No, I don't have any nephew at all."

"And I am also sure then that you would not have gone to Kolkata with Jasraj to attend a wedding," I said, as I stepped out from the main entrance.

"Not that I remember, Jeetu."

On the drive back home, I did not speak much. But my mind wandered a bit. What if we had not gone to that resort? What if Aashu had discussed the message from Jasraj with me? Did Anu actually take aim at Jasraj or did she want to kill Aashu? Did Jasraj actually have temporary amnesia or was he faking it? These were questions to which I knew I could never get answers. Not even from Ramky.

"Jeetu, are you going to leave that security person? He should have informed the police after the crime. And hence he is an accomplice."

Ramky wanted to go after somebody.

"Ramky, Manoj Pandey was only being a normal man wanting to feed his family. He probably didn't want to get caught in all this since his pistol was used to shoot. His family would have gone hungry for months before any justice would have prevailed. And knowing the clout of people like Jasraj and Anu here in India, he would have never got real justice. So, I don't blame him. And I genuinely forgive him."

"Jeetu, I am so glad to see you are still a good man at heart. Don't let anyone or anything change that."

Ramky patted me on the back.

Ramky left for Chennai later that night. He had called for a taxi from the company he was planning to invest in. I was so tired physically and emotionally that I hit the bed immediately after he left for the airport.

I woke up to a bright sunny day. And I was smiling. I knew the dream the previous night was not going to come true soon. But I had full faith in it coming true one day.

I recalled the dream again.

EPILOGUE

The year was 2069. I was sitting in an English literature class at a university in the US. We were discussing the romantic stories and epics of famous authors. There was a beautiful girl sitting next to me. She whispered to me softly, "Do you know that soulmates have a very low probability of meeting again in a human lifetime because you get only seven human lives from a total of 8.4 million lives?" I looked at her closely. She had light brown eyes. She looked at me and laughed. It was a laugh truly from the heart.

That was the last dream I ever remembered.

About the Author

Dhiraj Singh has successfully established and led several businesses in the infrastructure, services, and financial sectors in India and abroad. He is currently part of the senior leadership team at the largest Indian business support services group. Dhiraj holds a Master's degree in International Management from The American Graduate School of International Management, Thunderbird and an MBA in Finance from Tulane University, New Orleans. Dhiraj did his Bachelor's degree in Mechanical Engineering from the Indian Institute of Technology, Mumbai.

Born and brought up in a small town from where he travelled to study and work in different cities both in India and abroad, he has always excelled both in studies and sports while remaining a big movie buff! He is a keen observer of people from different cultural and social backgrounds and enjoys interacting with them and listening to their "stories". He has had major personal and spiritual transformation over the past decade due to many accurate astrological predictions and personal premonitions, including the death of his father, in his own life. Being an engineering and science student, he found the new “dimension” very baffling as well as interesting, and started to study and believe in “alternative science”, a science which he now believes exists but is not understood. His books in the series “Fables of Fatal Fate” are interesting fictional stories that are inspired by real life experiences and have a unique mix of drama and thrill creatively woven around the fabric of his “alternative science” views.

0270008460
150/-